Also by Ron Schwab

Adam's First Wife

The Law Wranglers

Ron Schwab

Uplands Press

OMAHA, NEBRASKA

Uplands Press
1401 S 64th Avenue
Omaha, NE 68106
www.uplandspress.com

Publisher's Note: This is a work of fiction. Names, characters, places, and incidents are a product of the author's imagination. Locales and public names are sometimes used for atmospheric purposes. Any resemblance to actual people, living or dead, or to businesses, companies, events, institutions, or locales is completely coincidental.

Ordering Information:
Quantity sales. Special discounts are available on quantity purchases by corporations, associations, and others. For details, contact the "Special Sales Department" at the address above.

Uplands Press / Ron Schwab -- 1st ed.

ISBN 978-1-943421-41-1

Adam's First Wife

The Law Wranglers

Chapter 1

JOSH RIVERS STOOD on the boardwalk outside the Rivers and Sinclair law office on The Plaza in Santa Fe. He felt strange wearing the wool suit and string tie clients expected a lawyer to wear in the town office and found himself longing for the informality of the firm's quarters near the Comanche reservation in Indian Territory. One of his partners, who also happened to be his wife, Jael Chernik Rivers, was speaking earnestly about something, but his attention had been captured by the sight of a woman mounted on a magnificent white stallion moving down the street in their direction. She was attired in a stunning red riding outfit, but her dark beauty would have made it impossible for any man who was not blind to avert his gaze, he thought. Their eyes met, and she gave him a quick smile and a nod. He smiled back and lifted his hat in greeting.

Josh's eyes followed the woman and the entourage of riders who trailed her, apparently heading north out of Santa Fe. He counted a half dozen men, including several he recognized as would-be gunslingers, but he took special note of the sinewy, towering man who rode beside her, whom he judged to be a mulatto. The man had a grim set to his mouth and had tendered a stony glare when Josh greeted the woman. Unfriendly sort. Likely devoid of a sense of humor.

"You haven't heard a word I've said, have you?" Jael asked.

He turned back to his wife. "What? I'm sorry. My mind was someplace else."

"Yes, I noticed. Someplace it shouldn't be. You're lucky that man didn't dismount and walk over here and bust your nose for ogling his woman."

"His woman? You think they're a pair? And I don't ogle."

"He thinks they are a pair. I'm not so sure about her. And you do ogle."

"I wonder who they are? I've never seen them before."

"Don't wonder. You've got a wife until you are widowed. A Comanche woman who does not share."

"You do know there is only one woman for me? My God, you're almost more than I can handle as it is."

"And I intend to keep it that way. Now, I was trying to tell you that Marty Locke has talked to Tara, and she has agreed to go with him to the Fort Sill office as soon as they are married next month. He will take over the routine business for the Comanche and Kiowa tribes. I will travel to the reservation at least twice a year to meet with Quanah and will go any other time he sends for me. Quanah is speaking English well enough now that communication should not be a problem, and Tara is committed to learning Comanche even though Marty will not promise."

"I guess it's settled then. We're permanent residents of the Santa Fe house and will work from the office here."

"I will miss my Comanche friends, but I am enthused. Michael will not have to switch schools every time we return to Fort Sill, and we will see more of Rylee now that we will be living here. And the law firm's growth demands more lawyers in this office."

"We really need to add a lawyer or two. Danna says she is keeping her eyes open for clerk prospects. Law school graduates want to stay in the big cities."

"You and Danna ended up in Santa Fe."

"Yes. But we both had roots in the Southwest. I grew up on the ranch in northern New Mexico Territory, and from the time I entered Hastings Law School in California, I knew I would come back this way. I doubt if I would have stayed with Dad on the ranch, though, even if Cassie hadn't been killed and Michael abducted. And Danna was a Texan and thought of the University of Virginia as a temporary detour. Then we caught Marty, another Virginia graduate, on the run from a tragic past. It seems like to get college-educated lawyers here, we've got to snag somebody with roots or catch a person running from something. Otherwise, we've got to make our own lawyers like we did with you. Danna thinks homemade are best and says the benefit of law school is highly overrated. I tend to agree."

"I am the most junior of the firm members, so I will let you and Danna worry about more lawyers. I will tell you about a concern of Danna's, though."

"What's that?"

"Keeping you in the office. She says you are still the name that attracts the lucrative clients, and, when you are in the office, you have no match in turning out the paperwork."

"But?"

"But you don't need much of an excuse to take you out of the office. You thrive on outdoor adventures that sometimes lead you into danger. Like working for Quanah when peace terms were being negotiated. You were only occasionally in the office for several years, she told me."

"Quanah paid us well . . . very well."

"And she does not deny that. But not all your quests pay. Even at Fort Sill, you jumped at any opportunity that necessitated travel. And as your wife, I like to have you home in my bed."

"I do like the last part." He looked down at her, searching her dark eyes. She was a tad less than five and a half feet tall, but at two inches over six feet, he still loomed over her. She was trying to be stern, likely at Danna's suggestion, but the dimple on her right cheek always betrayed her when she was less than serious. God, he loved this gorgeous Comanche Jewess. "Tell Danna I will try to stay closer to home." That was vague enough to give him some wiggle room, he figured. That issue settled as far as he was concerned, he wondered what that exotic-looking woman on the white stallion was up to.

Chapter 2

LILITH LA CROIX sat on her big white stallion, Lucifer, on a mountain bluff some eighty miles northwest of Santa Fe. She surveyed the lush green valley below, split by a winding ribbon of water tumbling over a rocky bed on its journey to the Chama River, which would spill it into the Rio Grande heading south across the territory toward Texas. Her lithe form, stretching nearly six feet in her black riding boots, cut an imposing figure in the saddle. She would reach her fortieth birthday in a few months but could easily pass for ten years younger, and she knew it. Lilith was attired in a scarlet, long-sleeved Mexican blouse and matching riding britches, and her sable hair flowed in swirls down her neck and dropped well below her shoulders. She routinely wore red-hued garments, thinking of the color as her trademark. She might concede to onyx set in silver for her jewelry now and then, but, usually, rubies were her preference.

She pointed to the hacienda tract with sprawling adobe house and outbuildings rising from the valley's west end against the backdrop of towering mountain peaks in the distance. "We found the sorry son-of-a-bitch," she said, her voice a near whisper. Only the tall, sinewy, man mounted on the sorrel gelding a few feet to her right could hear. "We'll take the trail back down the bluff and ride behind the hogback ridge that tapers off not far from the house. I don't want to take the place till after dark. We need to talk anyway."

There were seven riders. Besides Jacques "Jack" Moreau, her lifetime friend, longtime overseer and sometime lover, her two sons, twenty-one-year-old Raphael and nineteen-year-old Gabriel, had made the grueling trek from Louisiana with her. The other three were hired guns Jack had found in Santa Fe. They carried the monikers Pedro, Beast and Hugo, but Lilith did not know their surnames, and did not care, since they would likely have been invented anyway. Hugo was a pale, skinny man of medium height with reptilian eyes, who carried a six-shooter slung low on his hip and looked like he was coiled to strike. He claimed to be fast with a gun. They would see.

Beast's name fit. Blond with wind-burned fair skin, he was taller by several inches than Jack, who stood a good six-foot-three inches and weighed half again as much. He carried most of his thickness on a waist that lopped over his belt. He had a Peacemaker holstered at his side, but his weapon of choice was a sawed-off shotgun, which he cradled in several rawhide loops slung from his saddle horn.

Pedro was supposed to be the prize. A local Mexican, who claimed to be a vaquero, he appeared comfortable with the Winchester he carried in his scabbard and the Navy Colt tucked in the orange sash that circled his waist. But he was a small man who would not be much of a threat in a barroom brawl were it not for the wicked-looking knife sheathed and suspended from a leather thong below the sash. Jack had hired Pedro because the thirty-ish Mexican had once worked at the Bar P, the thirty-thousand-acre land grant spread formerly owned by Angelina Perez. She had inherited the property from her father, Miguel. The land grant was now titled in the name of Adam Laurent, who happened to be Lilith's husband and also claimed to be the spouse of Angelina Perez Laurent.

It was late afternoon when they staked their horses near a spring that trickled from a rocky escarpment and filled a stone-lined basin before spilling over and forming a tiny stream that fed the creek she had sighted earlier. Lilith noted that the natural bowl was large enough to bathe in, and she would have stripped and slipped into the icy water if it were not for the gawkers she rode with. That might not have deterred her if her sons were not present, Lilith thought, but even an immodest woman must draw some lines. Perhaps she would have invited Jack to join her.

The ridge shielded them from the sight of any cowhands working in the pastures or occupants of the hacienda grounds, but they could not risk a fire, so coffee would have to wait until they had finished their work. "Gabriel," she said, "get the hardtack and jerky from the packhorse. We'll eat now and talk of what we must do."

Gabriel, unfortunately, was his father's son in so many ways. Not so tall as she and Raphael and lighter-skinned, but so handsome he turned every woman's eye. Like Adam, he seemed unaware of his magnetism, and she suspected he was still a virgin. He seemed more enamored with books than young ladies, and his aspirations had leaned toward a professional education, perhaps law or medicine. Of course, he was so quiet and secretive, sometimes she had to admit she hardly knew him. She knew he feared her, and, unlike his brother, Gabriel was kind and weak and compliant. He had been devastated when Adam disappeared two years earlier. And despite his father's abandonment, he could not be trusted where Adam was concerned.

Raphael, on the other hand, was her son. He could be ice-cold and ruthless if the occasion called for it. Ambitious and single-minded in pursuit of wealth. He was not so handsome as his brother, but he was far from ugly. There was no kindness in him. And he probably had not been a virgin since he approached his fourteenth birthday. His appetite for the opposite sex, like her own, sometimes led him into dangerous waters. She thought it likely he had been sired by Jack, and Adam had accused her of just that. She had firmly denied the charge and savagely shredded his face with her talon-sharp fingernails for his words, but her denials fell just short of lies. Regardless, Raphael hated Adam, and she had no doubt he would kill the man he called "Father" if she asked. She would not. That would be her privilege when she was ready.

They gathered in the shade of a nearby aspen grove. Lilith claimed a flat-top boulder for her seat, and the others sat down on the rock and shale-covered ground and leaned against a tree or sat cross-legged facing her. Gabriel returned and began distributing the sorry meal.

Lilith vowed this would be the last time she would eat such crap.

As they ate, Lilith quizzed Pedro. "How many would you estimate might be on the place right now?"

"I think five, maybe six, besides Patron Adam and Señora Lauren . . . and girl, Margo. And cook, who also keeps casa."

"The sow's name is not 'Laurent.' She is not his wife. I am Adam's wife. His first wife. And only legal wife."

"I see, Señora. This I did not know. Forgive me."

"Where does Adam and his whore sleep?"

"Puta? Oh. West room. I never see this place, but I was one time in office, and a vaquero told me big bedroom is at hallway's stop. Girl and cook sleep in rooms at east side of casa."

"Do they post guards?"

"No more than one. Comanches on reservation. Apaches far away. No Indian troubles here. Have lookout, but he not look too much. Maybe sleep."

"Where would he be posted?"

"Near casa. Maybe on front veranda."

"That would be convenient. And the other hands would be in the bunkhouse?"

"Si, that is what I think."

"It seems almost too easy. I guess Adam was confident I wouldn't find him. He is such a fool. Very well, Pedro, after sundown, I want you to ride into the yard alone. When the guard challenges you, tell him you formerly worked on the ranch and are looking for a job. If you know the guard, just greet him like an old friend. Why did you leave the ranch in the first place?"

Pedro rolled his eyes and seemed to shrink into his billowy shirt and then cast his eyes on his scuffed boots. "It was the señorita's fault—the one who cooks and cleans. Consuelo. She begged for me to bed her, but when I please her, she say it was violacion."

"You raped her?"

"No, no. She want it. But her man finds us, and she screams. Say I make her do it. Not true. But he is foreman and beats me—sends me away. I would kill him. And take her again."

Lilith guessed there might be some truth to the Mexican's story, although she saw him as a likely rapist, if seduction failed. She had been raped at age fourteen, but before her fifteenth birthday, she had presided over the perpetrator's agonizing death and had stuffed the amputated genitals in his mouth before he took his last breath. A sixteen-year-old Jack had assisted with her first kill. It had been great fun.

"You can have the woman first, if you kill the guard without a shot being fired."

"Kill him?" Pedro shrugged. "Si, I can do that. With my blade."

"Jack and I will take the house while you and Gabriel stand guard outside the door. You will enter the house only when I call for you. Beast and Hugo will take the bunkhouse only after they see us go into the house. Raphael will go with them. Kill them all. No prisoners there. The girl, Margo, is my daughter. She would be fifteen now. You will not touch her. I will deal with her personally. We will let this Consuelo live for now. We can use a cook. After the house is secured, Pedro may have her for the first night. Any others who want her can draw straws to determine who gets her the next night and the following until you get a schedule set up."

"I want to see her first," grumbled Beast. "I don't want no pig."

Lilith ignored his remark. She figured the ugly barbarian had never had a woman he had not either paid for or raped. She did not trust the man and wondered if she would have to kill him sooner than she had planned.

"Nobody is being forced to use the woman. We will dispose of her eventually. She will know too much." She hoped the idiots would not reason out that they were also vulnerable to the same charge.

Beast said, "What happens when we kill all the cowhands? You seem to be looking to stay a spell. I ain't no cowboy."

"I didn't hire you to be a cowboy. You're a gun. I need you to help hold the place till the legal business is all worked out. Jack hired a half dozen cowhands—maybe a few more—who can use guns if they've got to. They should arrive within a few days. They'll tend to the ranching business, provide help for lookout shifts. The foreman is ex-Army. He'll organize defenses."

"Didn't sign on to be bossed by some soldier-type."

"Do you want to walk away from your money? Say so now."

"Well, no. I'll stick around and see how it works out."

This guy was trouble. She would use him for a while, but he was unlikely to live long enough to see his money.

Chapter 3

THE RIDERS WAITED in the shadows of a ravine that was carved out of the hacienda-side of the hogback ridge. Gabriel Laurent watched with apprehension as Pedro rode his black, white-stockinged gelding at a casual lope along a winding trail that led from the ridge to the ranch building site. He felt a chill and tugged his buckskin jacket tighter about his shoulders. It was mid-May, but after most of a lifetime in Louisiana, he was learning that the mountains at night tended to ignore the seasons. He loved the drier air here, though, and did not find himself longing for the humid Cajun country.

Gabriel considered the forthcoming reunion with his father. He was puzzled by the new wife mentioned so often by his mother, although he supposed his father could have divorced and remarried in two years' time.

His mother had learned of the new wife, but she insisted there had been no divorce and that any marriage was, therefore, null and void. When Adam Laurent had disappeared with his then thirteen-year-old daughter, Lilith La Croix had hired the Pinkerton Agency to locate her missing husband and daughter, and although the search had taken well over a year, the detectives had found him in New Mexico with a new wife and title to a substantial land grant.

Gabriel wanted no part of the reunion. He loved Adam Laurent and feared for his father's life. His mother was fierce and ruthless. He doubted she loved his father. He was unsure she loved anyone. People were possessions to her and dealt with as such. Adam Laurent was hers, and she intended to reclaim him and add to her financial holdings in the process. Her greed was boundless.

He could make out Pedro in the moonlight's glow. The Mexican had dismounted and was approaching the veranda when a man with a rifle stepped out of the shadows. The guard evidently recognized Pedro and lowered the weapon. A few minutes later, Pedro appeared to turn back to his horse but then wheeled and lunged toward the sentry, his arm swinging as he thrust the knife repeatedly. The man's knees buckled before his body collapsed on the ground in front of the attacker.

Lilith said, "Ride in quietly. Tie your horses on the corral fence. Then we'll split up and do our jobs."

Gabriel was hit by a sinking feeling in his gut, and his hands trembled as he mounted his coal-black gelding, the horse nearly invisible in the darkness. His mother would taunt him as a coward if she saw him shaking like this. But it was not anxiety for his own safety that tore at him. He knew that unspeakable things were on the agenda for this night, and he was helpless to put an end to it.

After they hitched the horses. Raphael headed for the bunkhouse with Beast and Hugo. Gabriel noted that his mother had taken the coiled bullwhip from the saddle horn. He shuddered, for he had felt its bite more than a few times. He followed Lilith and Jack to the house, where they were met on the veranda by Pedro.

"Don't get too full of yourself. You would have been a dead man if you had failed," Lilith said. "But, yes, you can have the woman tonight. Now, Gabriel, I've decided that you will enter the house with us. I may need you to calm your sister. Pedro, you will remain here as we planned. Fire your rifle if any problems come your way."

Jack opened the door and entered stealthily before nodding to Lilith, signaling she should join him. Gabriel slipped in behind them, surprised to find they were in a huge sitting room with an enormous stone fireplace furnished with ornate chairs and tables and stuffed, leather-covered couches, which he guessed were Spanish style. Adam Laurent was obviously living comfortably. He could not see his mother's face in the darkness, but he sensed her rage.

The room opened onto a hallway that ran east and west. Since the house front faced south, a left turn would take them past the office and to his father's bedroom. It felt obscene somehow to be sneaking up on the room where his father slept with his new wife. He hoped he would be assigned the other end of the hallway, where he might find Margo.

"Jack," Lilith said, "Find Margo's and the cook's rooms. Warn them to stay put. Gabriel, you will come with me."

Lilith moved swiftly and quietly down the hall, Gabriel following several paces behind and nervously pondering the scenarios that might play out when they confronted his father. He wished desperately that he had struck out on his own long before he had left New Orleans with his mother and Jack Moreau. He had an adequate stake of gold double eagles squirreled away in his saddle bags to make a fresh start someplace.

He caught a glimpse of the ranch office dimly lighted by moonbeams sifting through the window. And then they reached the hallway's end. It appeared there was a door directly to the outside of the house at the end of the hall. The room across from the office must be his father's. Lilith did not hesitate. She pushed the door open and stepped inside, her Colt in one hand and bullwhip in the other. "Out," she yelled. "Your hands to the sky, or I start squeezing the trigger."

When Gabriel came through the door, he could make out the outline of a four-poster bed in the dusky room and two shadowy figures pushing back covers and struggling to get up. "Light the lamp," Lilith barked.

"What the hell? Let us get something on."

"The whore goes down first. I can see her now. Light the lamp or she's buzzard bait."

"Okay. Okay." A match glowed, and Gabriel could see his father's shaky fingers fumbling with an oil lamp on the lampstand adjacent to the nearside of the bed. Adam adjusted the light to a soft radiance that revealed his naked form and that of a lovely woman with olive-brown skin, who was young enough to be his forty-five-year-old father's daughter. She was also naked but sat on the edge of the bed within reaching distance of Adam, a sheet tugged across her breasts and swollen belly, where she obviously carried a child. Her face was a mask of horror.

Lilith shrieked, "You pathetic son-of-a-bitch. You have not only been humping this harlot, you've got her with child."

Adam took a deep breath before he spoke, obviously trying to summon composure and a bit of dignity in his exposed condition. "Lilith, this woman is my wife, and I will not have you speaking of her this way. Now get the hell out of here and let us get dressed. We will all meet in the sitting room and discuss your visit like reasonable people."

Suddenly the roar of gunfire erupted from outside. Gabriel heard at least two shotgun blasts, and the reports of the Colts seemed endless. His father's eyes darted wildly, and his mother's lips formed a satisfied smile.

Adam bent over to retrieve his undershorts but stumbled forward and almost fell when the bullwhip cracked, and the tail slashed a bloody gash across his hip and buttocks. The young woman screamed and ducked away but not before she took a lash across her back. Lilith quickly turned her attention back to Adam, and the whip's tail struck his shoulder before he righted himself. Gabriel could see his mother had slipped into one of her frenzies. She would wield the whip until his father's flesh was shredded to the bone.

He grabbed his mother's arm, aborting her next strike. Adam lunged and grabbed the whip's tail, yanking it sharply and pulling it from Lilith's hand.

She turned and attacked Gabriel, raking her razor-edged fingernails across the bridge of his nose and clawing at his face, hysterical with rage. "You milksop, you yellow-bellied, ball-less coward."

"Mother. Stop. Calm yourself." He could not bring himself to strike back, so he dodged and weaved, trying to avoid her onslaught. Finally, Adam, his undershorts pulled on now, latched his arms about Lilith's waist and dragged her away.

"Lilith, for God's sake, control yourself. We've got to talk."

"Let go of me you . . . you fence-jumping bastard."

Then Jack Moreau appeared seemingly from nowhere, and Gabriel saw the mulatto's arm arc downward with the butt of the pistol aimed for the back of Adam's skull. Gabriel flinched at the thud that dropped his father to the floor.

Moreau spoke softly to Lilith, calming her like a man might a frightened and resisting horse. "Get hold of yourself, Lilith. Settle down now. We've got work to be doing." He kneaded her shoulders and raked his long fingers through her thick hair, brushing his lips against her ear as he whispered to her.

Gabriel thought Jack Moreau was the only sentry who stood between his mother and total insanity. He had always been a presence in their household, residing in a small cottage, a renovated slave's quarters, near the colonial mansion just a few miles outside New Orleans. As a child, Gabriel had thought of Jack as a kindly uncle, but as he grew older, he came to realize the relationship with his family was more complex. He had no doubt that Jack was his mother's frequent lover and that the lives of the two were deeply intertwined. Why had she not just married her childhood friend and saved his father all the grief and pain of a tormented marriage? Of course, there would have been no Gabriel or Margo. Raphael, he was not so certain about.

Gabriel knelt by his father. The back of Adam's head was blood smeared. He appeared semi-conscious and breathed steadily. Gabriel glanced over at the young woman, who leaned against the far wall with the sheet wrapped about her body, her head lowered. She sobbed but not hysterically. She appeared to be collecting herself. That was good. Lilith fed off others' fear and hysteria, which served as a trigger for even more violence.

Lilith seemed to have collected her composure now and assumed command again. "We will wait till morning to sort this out. The woman, of course, cannot be allowed to birth the bastard she's carrying, but she might be useful for a few days to encourage Adam's cooperation. Jack, put the whore in Margo's room and bring Margo back here for a chat. After that, she and the slut can bunk together."

"Do you want a guard on their door?"

"No, that's not necessary. Where would they go? They're miles from a neighbor or any town. And, Gabriel, you'll sleep in the stable. If anybody leaves this place with a horse, you will face a lashing you likely will not survive. Understand?"

"Yes, Mother." He did not doubt she could devour her own young if provoked, like some animals.

"As for Adam, Gabriel, fetch Beast and Hugo to come get your father. When they have cleared the bunkhouse of the corpses, they can stay with him in there, take watch shifts. You can put up all the horses. If there isn't room for all of them in the stable, put the extra in the corral. Does that frighten you too much?"

He did not reply to her sarcastic arrow. He walked out of the room and down the hallway, taking note of the location of rooms at the other end before making a turn and walking through the sitting room toward the veranda.

Chapter 4

AFTER BEAST AND Hugo dragged Adam away, Lilith paced the floor, waiting for Jack to return with Margo. When he finally appeared with her daughter, Lilith found herself almost disbelieving that the wide-eyed creature who entered the room was the daughter who had run off with Adam two years earlier. That had been a gangly, flat-chested skinny-legged girl. This was a young woman not quite fully blossomed but on the edge of mature beauty. Her figure had filled out in the right places, and she had grown an inch or two, still leaving her several inches shorter than her exceptionally tall mother. Lilith was pleased that her daughter's smoothly carved facial features and coloring favored her own, but it had always grated on her that the girl had her father's gentle soul.

Margo was biting her lower lip nervously, and her fingers clung to a green, cotton robe as she eyed her mother uncertainly with those dark haunting eyes. No emotional grand reunion here. Margo was afraid. Good. She should be. There would be a price to pay for her rebellion.

"Shall I leave the two of you together for a private chat?" Jack asked.

"Yes," Lilith replied. "Check on the men. Be sure they've got Adam under guard. Tell Raphael he's posted on the veranda for the night and that Pedro will relieve him a few hours before sunrise. Instruct Pedro to take his woman if he wants her but to finish in time to relieve Raphael. Then return here. We're spending the night in this room."

Jack gave her a knowing smile. "Whatever you say, boss lady."

After Jack departed, Margo and Lilith stood facing each other for several moments before Lilith stepped over to her daughter and smacked the girl's face sharply with the palm of her hand. Then she swung her arm back and struck her below the eye with a closed fist. Margo stumbled backward several paces but did not cry out, a switch from several years earlier when she would have been bawling like a baby. Lilith had mixed feelings about this, glad that her daughter was exhibiting some toughness, concerned that Margo was not going to be so malleable.

"I am so pleased to see you, too, Mother," Margo said sarcastically.

Lilith slapped her again. "Don't smart-mouth me, bitch."

Margo said nothing.

"Why did you leave with your father? He couldn't have taken you if you had raised a fuss."

"He told me he was leaving. He said he would like to take me with him if I wanted. I said I wanted."

"But why? You had everything there. The finest clothes. Servants. The promise of a large inheritance someday."

"And I have never been happier than I have been the past two years. I haven't missed you for a minute, Mother."

Lilith raised her hand to slap her daughter again and then thought better of it. "Well, I am here to stay, so you had better be changing your attitude. Your father's whore will be departing, and I am assuming my rightful place as his wife."

"You are no longer Father's wife. Angelina is his wife. She is good to him. And to me. She is like sister and mother to me."

This time, Lilith could not restrain herself. She lunged at Margo and began hammering on her with her fists. "You ungrateful, traitorous bitch. Your Angelina is a dead woman. You are mine, and I am here to stay. Get used to it."

Margo finally pushed her mother back and ducked away, rushing for a wide chest of drawers opposite the foot of the bed. She reached into the center top drawer and withdrew a Colt Peacemaker, leveling it at Lilith. "Father taught me how to use this, Mother, and told me where I could find it. I prefer not to kill you, but I am capable of doing so if it will save Father and me."

Lilith stared at Margo in disbelief. The girl had some backbone, and her eyes said she would fire the damn thing. It was time to back off. This was not the whimpering little mouse she had brought up in the Louisiana mansion. There would be ample opportunity to deal with her rebellion another time. She stepped backward with her hands half-raised placatingly. "Don't get excited, Margo, but you must understand that you can have only one mother. And I am the one who bore the pain to bring you into this world. It hurts me for you to deny this."

Margo still gripped the Peacemaker tightly, but Lilith could see the girl's resolve weaken just a bit. She had always given in easily to guilt that made her vulnerable to manipulation. Margo and Gabriel both carried too much of their father's blood. There was only one mistake she would concede making in her lifetime—the choosing of Adam Laurent to sire her children. Two of them, anyway.

"There is more to being a mother than giving birth."

"I am willing to talk about this another day. Perhaps we can yet become friends. But you cannot seriously believe I am not your father's wife?"

"Not in the eyes of God. Father and I have been baptized and taken instruction. We have been confirmed as members of the Roman Catholic Church. Father and Angelina were married by a priest in Santa Fe. You and Father were not married in the Church. The Church does not recognize your marriage."

Lilith fought to control herself. She could not slap any sense into the pious little twit while she held the gun. "But the law, not the Church, determines if a marriage is legal. Your father is a bigamist. I am his first and only wife."

"God is higher than the law, and He says Angelina is Father's wife." Margo stepped slowly toward the door with the pistol still aimed at Lilith's chest. "I am returning to my room. Angelina is there. I must talk to her. Anyone who enters without knocking will be shot."

After Margo departed, Lilith sat down on the bed. She did not like this business of Margo possessing a gun. That would have to be remedied in the morning. Perhaps she would send one of the dispensable ones, like Beast, through the door first to test her daughter's resolve. Regardless, tomorrow she would bring some order to this place.

She undressed and crawled beneath the sheets to wait for Jack. She would be unable to sleep without him. Fortunately, he returned within a half hour. When he stepped into the room, she pushed back the covers to reveal herself. "Hurry," she said, "we will talk later."

Chapter 5

GABRIEL HAD UNSADDLED the horses and given them a light brushing down before giving each a dash of grain and tossing hay in each stall. Fortunately, there was a water pump just outside the stable section of the huge barn, but it had been serious work pumping and carrying the water two buckets at a time to fill the small metal tanks in each stall. The stable included twenty stalls, an even larger capacity than the plantation's, and, even with the horses his party had ridden, only a dozen of these were occupied. He assumed other ranch horses grazed in a pasture nearby and that the remuda for the next day's work was kept in the stable.

There were some fine animals here. He gathered these were working cow horses, where those back home, except for the draft horses, had been utilized for transport from plantation to town or to oversee the fieldwork by the now emancipated Negroes. He loved horses and was proud that his friends considered him a superior judge of fine horseflesh.

His orders were to stay in the stable for the night. It was midnight now, and he could not risk wasting more time. He was determined to check on his father's condition and hoped to seek his advice.

Gabriel strode to the bunkhouse where Adam Laurent had been incarcerated. He rapped softly on the door.

"Who is it?" The gravelly voice belonged to Beast.

"Gabriel. My mother sent me," he lied.

The door opened, and Gabriel entered the cramped room filled with eight narrow beds, no more than two feet between each. Hugo slept on a bed near the doorway, although Gabriel had no doubt the gunfighter would awaken in an instant if trouble threatened. Adam Laurent sat on a straw-filled mattress on one of the beds furthest from the door, elbows on his knees and his chin cradled in his hands. Blood dripped from the back of his scalp onto the neck of an already saturated shirt. He looked up, raised his head, and his eyes brightened when he saw Gabriel squeezing between the rows of beds and taking a seat facing him on the side of the adjacent bed.

"French or Spanish?" Gabriel asked. All family members were fluent in both languages in addition to English.

"Le Francais." Continuing in French, Adam said, "I think Hugo understands some Spanish. I do not know how much, but the things we must speak of are not for other ears."

"You are obviously in pain, Father. Can I do something?"

"No. My head is clearing. I am much better now that you are here. I am trying to collect my thoughts now. They killed all the cowhands in the bunkhouse. You can see the bloody mess here. They dragged the bodies out back. I suppose they will bury them in the morning. These were good, hard-working men, and they were slaughtered like butcher hogs. Some were asleep, I think. But I suppose that was a blessing."

"I knew mother would bring hell to your life if she found you. At first, I refused to go with her, but I relented, because I wanted to see you and Margo again."

"I should have asked you to leave New Orleans with us. But I thought you were old enough to protect yourself and capable of being on your own. And I did not know where we were going to end up. But I figured it would not be near educational opportunities, and you always said you wanted to get more education and strike out on your own—do something outside the family businesses. I intended to find you someday and inform you of our whereabouts. And I had no time to warn you. Your mother had beaten Margo nearly senseless the day before. You were on a hunting trip with your friend, Crawfish."

"Yes. And when I came back, you and Margo were gone."

"The next day, I cleaned every dollar I had out of the banks. I didn't touch the business accounts, so it wasn't all that much. But I had a stake. Most of the lands and town properties were in your mother's name, and she is a wealthy woman. I hoped she wouldn't look too hard for us. I was wrong. She's Lilith, descendant of Adam's first wife. Nobody crosses her. That's why she married me, you know—because of my first name. She thought it was destiny. And she can cast a magic spell on a man when she chooses. I am not sorry because, if we had not married, you and Margo would not be."

Gabriel noted Adam's omission. "You did right to take Margo away. I am confused about the new wife and the ranch you have here, but all I care about is the safety of you and Margo. Mother says I am weak. Perhaps she is correct. But I will do whatever I can to help you."

"You are not weak. Believe that. Hate and cruelty are not courageous. Violence is not bravery. But some of us thrive only amidst peace. I was not strong enough to live out my life in a constant state of war with your mother. And I feared for Margo's well-being. If there is a coward, it is I, for I ran."

Gabriel had to ponder his father's last remark. He studied his father's face. He was still a handsome man, a few more lines in his lightly bronzed skin, the heritage of a northern Sioux wife taken by one of his French ancestors. His black hair revealed a few flecks of gray, but he remained lean and fit, and Gabriel decided that forty-five might not be as ancient as he once thought. Adam's dark eyes were what haunted the son. They were windows to deep despair. "What would you have me do, Father?"

"It involves great risk."

"I am willing to take whatever risk is needed." He did not hesitate. Unlike his mother, his father would never ask him to do something that would violate his conscience.

"Can you get Margo and Angelina out of the house?"

"I think so. They share a room. I do not think there is a guard. Where is Margo's room?"

"North side of the hallway. First door."

"There will be a guard on the veranda. Perhaps Raphael."

"Would you be able to strike your brother? With the butt of your pistol, for instance?"

Gabriel thought about this. He had engaged in more than a few fisticuffs with his brother over the years, consistently ending up on the losing end of the tussle. He did not relish the notion of an unprovoked attack but replied, "I can do that." Certainly, Raphael would never anticipate his little brother having the gumption to initiate an assault.

"Angelina will be killed. Your mother has said as much. Your sister's life with your mother would be unbearable. You must take them away from here. To Santa Fe. Tell the United States Marshal there what has happened here."

"But what about you, Father?"

"There is nothing you can do for me. The two guards cannot be dealt with without alerting the others. And we would be no match for their guns. Your mother has plans for me. She will not have me killed immediately. Hopefully, the law will arrive before she is finished with me. You must see to Margo and Angelina."

"Mother will follow. She will send her men after us."

"I am asking you to take great risk. But Angelina and Margo are not helpless. Both are trained in the use of rifles and Margo is proficient with any revolver and keeps a double-barreled shotgun under her bed. Your sister is not the child you knew. She carries your mother's strength and toughness but does it with a kind heart. And you can do this. Disregard your mother's judgment. You are a brave and resourceful young man, and you will come to know this soon. I do worry about Angelina and the baby, but they will die here if she stays. There is no choice. She must leave."

"I do not know this country, Father. I can find the trail we came on. Much of it seems heavily travelled, but I fear we would be easily found."

"No, you are correct. You must take the river route. Follow the stream that cuts through the valley. It will take you south to the Chama River. Follow the trails along the river—some will take you through high country with steep canyon walls, but there are rocks and caves to hole up in if you must. It may take two to three days travel, but you will reach a fork where the Chama joins the Rio Grande flowing from the northeast on its journey south. You should find a crossing here that will take you to the Santa Fe-Taos road. You were in Santa Fe, yes?"

"Yes. Mother had business there. We stayed three nights. That is where Jack hired his gunfighters and a ranch crew."

"Then you would have taken that road at the beginning of your journey here. Many people travel on this road, which should afford some protection. A long day's ride from the fork should see you in Santa Fe . . . unless—"

"Unless what?"

"Unless Angelina has difficulty with your journey. The baby is due in a month. It could be sooner. The trip will be rugged and difficult for a woman in her condition. You may have to stop and let her rest often. You do not know her, Son, but she is a fine woman. Margo will watch her closely, but I trust you to consider her needs. The child she carries is your half-brother or sister."

Gabriel felt no kinship to either woman or child, but he was driven to take his sister from this place, and he felt duty-bound to honor his father's wishes. "I will do my best, Father."

"Hey. That's enough. Talk American if you're going to keep talking."

Gabriel tossed a look over his shoulder and saw that Beast was glaring at them, obviously becoming uneasy with the French conversation. "I am sorry," Gabriel said, with a contriteness he did not feel. "My father speaks more easily in French. He can barely speak English."

The statement elicited a doubtful look. "Well, finish up and be on your way."

Gabriel turned back to Adam and, speaking in French again, said, "I have work to do, Father. I must go."

"Yes, you must. I will pray for you, Gabriel. May God ride with you. Whatever happens, know that I love you. And if things do not go well, tell Angelina and Margo that I said I would love them to my last breath."

Gabriel stood, placed his hand on his father's shoulder and bent over and kissed him softly on the forehead. "And I love you, Father. I will try to bring help soon."

Chapter 6

WHEN GABRIEL STEPPED out of the barn, he tucked the handle of the blacksmith's hammer into his belt and tugged his buckskin jacket over it, hoping his brother would not notice the bulge underneath. He had never hit a man with the butt of a pistol before and had been nervous about how much force to apply to take a man down. He was confident the hammer's heavy iron head was up to the task, though. He just did not want to kill Raphael. The mere thought of striking his sibling made his stomach queasy.

He had selected three fresh horses from the stable, two geldings for Margo and himself and a gentle mare for Angelina, and the mounts were saddled and ready to ride. He had led another mare out of a stall for packhorse service or to serve as a backup mount. There was little to pack beyond his own bedroll. He would try to retrieve blankets for his companions from the house. He had several canteens, and they would be riding near water, so drink for people and critters should not be a problem. Food for the riders could be troublesome. He carried fishing hooks and line in his saddlebags, and during the trip from Santa Fe he had noted a fair amount of game. But could they risk a fire? And, certainly, gunfire could be a giveaway to any pursuers. Perhaps Margo and Angelina could scavenge quietly in the house before they departed.

He had cut a half dozen four-foot lengths of a rope and slung them over his shoulder and made no effort to conceal his approach as he sauntered toward the veranda. Raphael sat slouched on the steps, smoking a cigarette, seemingly disinterested as his brother drew nearer. When Raphael looked up, he eyed the ropes and hammer with curiosity. "What in the hell are you up to, Chucklehead?"

"This," Gabriel said, as he raised the hammer and drove it into the side of his brother's head, striking just above his left ear. He winced at the thud and Raphael's grunt, just before his brother toppled over and landed on the shale pathway. He knelt and placed his hand on Raphael's back to confirm he was still breathing. Raphael breathed, but it was shallow. Gabriel had no idea whether that was good or bad, but at least he was alive at this moment, though it did not appear he would regain consciousness anytime soon.

He dragged the prostrate form off the path and hog-tied his hapless quarry with several of the rope lengths, pulling Raphael's hands behind his back and anchoring the wrists to one ankle. Then he gagged him with a kerchief pressed between Raphael's teeth and tied tightly behind the back of the neck. He gave up on shaking off the guilt he felt for the assault on his brother. They had never been close, and Raphael had never passed up an opportunity to torment or put Gabriel down. But still, they were brothers, and that counted for something. In his own mind, anyway; not likely in Raphael's.

With Raphael secured, Gabriel slipped through the doorway, still carrying the blacksmith's hammer, and crept across the parlor, taking a left turn when he reached the hallway. He knew Margo's room was to the right, but the sound of sobbing and coughing coming from the room on the other side of the hall distracted him. He paused and moved to the closed door, pressing his ear to the door and listening. Silence. He knew Pedro was in the room with the young Mexican cook. His commitment was to aid the escape of his sister and his father's new wife. But the sobs had touched his conscience, and he did not know if he had the toughness to walk away. He had to decide quickly.

The decision was made for him when the door opened, and a surprised, wide-eyed Pedro stood there. Reflexively, Gabriel swung the hammer with all the force he could muster, striking the Mexican gunslinger above the eye, the crunch of bone signaling success before Pedro fell backwards into the bedroom. Gabriel thought his proficiency with the hammer was improving with each blow and determined that the former tool, now weapon, was going to be added to his armaments. He stepped into the room, kicking Pedro's legs aside to clear the path for closing the door.

Gabriel caught sight of the naked woman sprawled atop the bed with her head twisted at a strange angle in a backdrop of blood-soaked blankets. He rushed to the bedside already certain the young woman was dead. He leaned over and saw that her throat had been cut almost to the point of decapitation of her head, and he quickly turned away, gagging and swallowing back the vomit rising in his throat. He stepped over to the still form crumpled on the floor and found himself wanting to take the hammer and pound Pedro's head to mush. But he had spent his short lifetime controlling the rage that he had seen so often vented by his mother, and he refused to give in to it.

He knelt and felt the Mexican's chest. He was not certain whether he was alive or dead. Any breathing was imperceptible. Had he killed a man? If so, the world had suffered no loss. But Gabriel had never killed a man, and he took no satisfaction in it if, in fact, he had.

Enough. He had a mission, and every minute was important. He got up and headed across the hall to Margo's room, closing the door behind him. He tapped softly on his sister's door. He heard footsteps approaching the door.

"Who is it?" Margo's voice responded.

"Gabriel," he said in a soft voice. He heard a click of the door bolt. Margo opened the door a crack, and when she saw him, she pulled it back to admit him and lowered the Colt that she held in her hand. As soon as he entered, she closed the door and pushed the bolt back into place.

She turned and looked at him uncertainly before he smiled. "I've missed you, Sis," he said.

Instantly, she rushed into his arms, taking care to point the pistol away. "Oh, Gabe. I've missed you, too. You can't imagine how much. I didn't think I would ever see you again."

After clinging to him for several moments, Margo stepped back, not attempting to hide the tears sliding down her cheeks. She was not her mother's daughter, Gabriel thought. He had never seen his mother cry. But Margo had shed her coltish form and cherubic face and was on the verge of blossoming into a striking beauty. "We cannot delay. I have come to take you away from here. You and father's—" He looked at the wide-eyed, petite woman sitting on the edge of the bed with a satiny yellow robe clutched over a seriously pregnant belly.

"Wife." Margo finished his sentence for him. She gestured for the young Mexican woman to join them. "Gabe, this is Angelina, Father's wife and our stepmother. Angelina, this is my brother, Gabriel—I call him 'Gabe.'"

The woman Margo called stepmother was not many years older than himself, but Gabriel removed his hat and offered a slight bow, feeling a bit silly with his hat in one hand and the big hammer in the other. "My pleasure, ma'am. Sorry about the circumstances."

Angelina approached warily and said, "Your father speaks of you with great pride and affection. He has missed you."

Margo interrupted the awkward meeting, rescuing him from a struggle with polite conversation. "Gabriel, how did you find us? What is happening? What is Mother going to do?"

"Mother hired the Pinkerton Agency to find you. They are obviously very capable. Mother intends to take over this ranch. She insists she is still Father's wife and that he is an adulterer and bigamist. She would phrase this in more profane terms, of course."

"But she cannot just ride in here and evict the rightful owners. The law will not allow it."

"I have never known that to stop Mother. But we are wasting time. I have spoken with Father. He says I am to take both of you away from here. Tonight. He believes Angelina's life is in danger, and under no circumstances will the baby be allowed to live."

"I can't believe Mother would kill them."

"Are you certain of that?"

She did not reply, and that answered his question.

"But where would we go? They will follow us."

"Santa Fe. You will be safe there, and we can notify the United States Marshal. The law will take care of this."

"Can you find the way?"

"Father told me what to do. But we can't waste time. The horses are saddled. You must dress for the trip. I have some ropes stuffed in my coat pocket. If you will give me some blankets and extra clothing, I will prepare bedrolls for both of you."

"Consuela," Margo said. "We cannot leave her here. These men will do terrible things to her. And Mother will not let her live."

"I'm sorry. She is dead. A man named Pedro killed her. They are in her bedroom. I took him down with my hammer. I don't know if he will live. He claimed he worked here once."

Angelina burst into tears. "She was my friend. Ever since we were children. Her mother cared for the casa, and her father was foreman for the rancho. They were killed during the same Apache raid that took my mother. She was ten, and I was eleven at the time. She made her home with us, and my father raised us as sisters. She and Juan were to be married."

"Juan was one of the cowhands?"

"Yes," Angelina said.

"I'm sorry to tell you they are all dead."

"I must sit down," Angelina said, as she returned to the bed. "I do not understand. Why?"

Gabriel said, "Revenge for a start. But Lilith never passes up the opportunity to convert a grievance to dollars. She has it in her head she's going to own this ranch. Of course, once that's nailed down, she will sell it and return to Louisiana, unless she decides to leave Raphael here to run the operation. I am sorry I must give you this bad news, but we must go now."

Margo said, "I have this Colt, and there is a double-barreled shotgun under the bed. There are cartridges and loaded shotgun shells in the bottom-right dresser drawer. I've got denim riding britches and boots I'll slip on. But Angelina's clothes are in the bedroom where Mother is at—with Jack, I assume," she added with more than a hint of sarcasm. "Angelina would not fit into my britches in her present condition, and I'm ten inches taller. I suppose we could get one of my dresses over her and cut some of the skirt bottom off. She'll need something on her feet. I have a pair of moccasins, but her tiny feet will swim in them."

"Just put together what you can."

"I know. Consuela was closer to Angelina's size. I'll get some things from her room."

She started for the door, but Gabriel stepped in front of her. "I'll see what I can scavenge. You get yourself dressed and gather up what you can."

When Gabriel entered Consuela's room, he noted that Pedro had not moved but seemed to be breathing regularly. He had ample rope, so he tied the man's hands behind his back and gagged him with a scarf he found on a coat hook. The rapist-murderer deserved death, but Gabriel could not bring himself to wield the hammer. He found a few dresses and a pair of moccasins and a quilt in the closet. He was not sure about the undergarments, so he plucked an assortment from the chest-of-drawers, avoiding anything frilly or ballooning.

He returned to Margo's room and found his sister attired like a cowboy from slouch-hat to boots, although leaving little doubt that a leggy, young woman was hidden underneath the garments. She even had her Colt holstered on a cartridge belt fastened above her hips. A young Lilith but, thank God, without the twisted mind. Angelina was stripping the bed of blankets and had folded several, which rested atop a big oak chest with a shotgun and box of shells.

Gabriel tossed his collection of clothing articles on the bed. "Angelina, this is the best I could come up with. We're going to be riding, and there were not any side saddles in the barn. I'll turn my back to you and take a few of the blankets and make up bedrolls, while you ladies figure out how to dress you up for the ride."

Gabriel was pleased to discover there were five wool blankets, so he disqualified the goose-down quilt and assigned two of the less bulky wool covers to each of the bedrolls. He knelt and folded them and rolled them up, cinching them tightly with his remaining rope

"Turn around and look," Margo said.

Gabriel got up and could not suppress a grin when he saw the dressmakers' handiwork. Poor Angelina looked like a clown at the New Orleans Mardi Gras. They had pulled a gingham dress over her enceinte body but to make room for her protruding belly, they had slit the front that now revealed an egg-shaped bulge covered by a white chemise. They had taken scissors to the skirt and made pantlegs by wrapping the fabric around Angelina's limbs and anchoring it with rags. At least the moccasins fit, he thought.

"Now, can you find some coats? Then we make a quick stop at the kitchen, and after that we hit the trail."

"What about guards?"

"Raphael and Pedro are sleeping, and everyone else is otherwise occupied."

Chapter 7

OLIVER WOLF REMOVED the canvas from the easel when he was satisfied the paints were dry. He placed it on top of four other paintings spread out on the naked granite bluff and then gently rolled them up and slid them into a cylindrical leather case which would be anchored to the packhorse for the return journey to Santa Fe. There, in the light of his studio, he would do the touch-up work before delivery to the customers, who had purchased the works sight unseen. During his two-week trek into the mountains above the Chama River valley, he had also sketched a dozen scenes that would inspire additional landscape paintings before being sold to art lovers who collected sketches. Commissioned portraits had constituted the initial demand for his work, that and his horse and wildlife penciled drawings. Now the local demand for anything he did was seemingly insatiable.

After he secured his supplies, gear, and artwork on the packhorse, Wolf saddled Owl, his big, coal-black stallion, named for the irregular white circles that framed his eyes and gave the animal an owlish look. A few splotches of what looked like spilled whitewash frosted the muscular horse's rump to make his appearance even more distinctive. Wolf walked to the edge of the precipice to take a final look at the breathtaking panorama of the Chama over a thousand feet below, snaking its way through the narrow, colorful sandstone-walled canyon. Turning his eyes upward, he took in the towering snow-covered peaks in the distance still refusing to concede that spring had arrived. He never tired of the breathtaking spectacle. He had been raised in eastern Indian Territory and western Arkansas, where mountains were molehills compared to these of northern New Mexico Territory. And his war years as a major in the First Cherokee Brigade of the Confederate Army had taken him nowhere to compare to this artist's dream.

He started to turn away when he caught a glimpse of objects moving on a trail that threaded through the rocks on a wide ledge some hundred feet above the canyon floor. Riders, he decided, moving faster than good sense called for. He retrieved his mariner's telescope from a leather bag looped over his saddlehorn and returned to his perch. He pressed the telescope to his eye and focused. Three riders, moving single file, the one in the middle a woman, signaled by her billowy garments and the orange scarf wrapped over her head. The rider bringing up the rear and leading a packhorse was male, but Wolf was uncertain about the front rider. Low crowned hat with hair tied back and dropping over shoulders. Lithe form but mostly covered by a deerskin coat. But there was something about the set of the rider in the saddle that suggested female. She was clearly the most comfortable rider of the three.

They were moving with foolhardy speed, begging for a spill that would launch a rider over the canyon wall or cause a stumble on the rock and shale trail that would break a horse's leg. Oliver Wolf, known as White Wolf in another life, loved horses even more than his art and was more disturbed by thought of an injury to a mount than the demise of some nameless stranger.

The riders behaved like they were being chased by a pack of angry wolves. He wondered about that and roamed the telescope back up the trail. He soon spotted the pursuers. There were two riders, one a large, big-bellied man, who lagged some distance behind the other, probably because of the burden the bay horse was forced to carry. Regardless, it was high noon now. The chasers were moving at a slower pace, but each had a spare horse in addition to a packhorse they shared.

But the pursued would be forced to rest their horses soon. Also, the woman leaned forward in the saddle like she was having difficulty keeping up the pace. She obviously was not a strong rider. He figured the men who followed would easily catch the leaders within two hours.

Wolf sighed. What was it to him? While he had his instinctive suspicions, he could not be certain who the good guys were and who the bad guys were. The only law hereabouts was United States Marshal Chance Calder, and he knew neither of the trailing riders was Chance. Wolf served as a reluctant, occasional deputy for Marshal Calder only because of the bond they had formed three or four years back when Chance was top sergeant and Wolf served as a civilian scout for Colonel Ranald Slidell Mackenzie during the Red River War. He carried on a quick debate with himself and lost.

The distance was too great for him to intercept the leading riders before the others caught up. The best he could do was find a trail that led to the canyon floor and move into better rifle range. He wouldn't have to go all that far since his saddle scabbard carried his old Army

Sharps that had an effective firing range of five hundred yards. A marksman could hit a target at a half mile. He was a marksman.

Wolf led the horses down the backside of the bluff, weaving through the pine and aspen until the slope leveled off some onto a small meadow that was lush with awakening grasses. He staked Owl and the packhorse and retrieved his Sharps. He grabbed an empty canvas bag with a braided leather shoulder strap and dropped some cartridges and the telescope in it before leaving the horses to graze. At the meadow's edge, he picked up a deer trail that veered in the direction of the canyon wall. It was a well-used trail that did not test his tracking skills and took him quickly to the canyon's rim. He was pleased to find that the trail widened here, and the slope was not unduly steep. Horses could negotiate the pathway, and he suspected Apache and Comanche, perhaps even Navajo or Pueblo, had made their descents here many times over at least several centuries. He staked his horses in the meadow and hurried on foot down the trail.

A bit more than halfway down the canyon wall, he came to a cluster of boulders, the largest reaching nearly waist high and resting on the trail's edge overlooking the canyon. Wolf reached over his shoulder and plucked the telescope from the bag and moved behind the boulder to survey the other side of the canyon. As he had guessed, the three riders had stopped on the trail. The fools had ridden the horses too hard, and if they tried to push the animals anymore, they would soon be afoot. It would serve them right, but he was not going to tolerate the suffering of the mounts.

They were sitting on the ground, seemingly oblivious to the pursuers. A lookout had not even been posted. Now that he was nearer, he could see that there were two women, one quite young and the other carrying a child. The male looked to be closer to boy than man. He moved the telescope back up the canyon until the followers came into view. They were closing the gap quickly now. In fifteen minutes, they would catch up with their quarry. He needed to alert the young people that danger was imminent. He could easily drop the pursuing riders with a few shots from the Sharps, but he was reluctant given he did not know the story that was playing out on the other side of the narrow canyon. He readied the Sharps and squeezed the trigger, aiming at no specific target. The rifle's roar echoed off the canyon's walls and likely sounded like a cannon to the uninitiated.

The young man snatched up his rifle, and the girl stood up with a gun—evidently a shotgun—cradled in her arms. The two men reined in their horses, and Wolf delivered a dose of lead through the big man's hat. That got their attention, and they wheeled their horses and headed northwest back up the trail. He continued a rain of fire, taking care not to strike man or horse but sending the message that his range was long and that he could take them down if he chose. Finally, he ceased firing and picked up the telescope, his eye trailing them as they continued their retreat. They showed no signs of stopping or regrouping to take up the chase again, at least not anytime soon. He turned away and started his climb back up the trail to retrieve the horses, hopeful he could ride Owl down the same route to the canyon floor. A river crossing would be necessary to reach the other side of the canyon floor, but the Chama was not a formidable river this far north. It was time to meet the greenhorns who drew him into this bit of unpleasantness.

Wolf easily located a widening in the river that offered good footing on a shale bed beneath shallow water that allowed crossing without any threat to his sketches and paintings. He urged Owl up a trail that connected with that followed by the three riders. Within a half hour he reached the clearing where the greenhorns had collected the good sense to wait. They watched him warily as he approached, the young man gripping a Winchester with barrel pointed toward the ground, but a tall girl was holding a double-barreled shotgun aimed directly at his chest.

He reined in some twenty-five feet distant. "I'm not looking for trouble. I thought we'd talk a spell. But if I'm not welcome here, I'll just turn back and be on my way."

"Wait, mister," the young man said. He turned to the girl. "Margo, lower your damned shotgun." Then, speaking to Wolf, "I think we should talk."

Oliver nodded and dismounted, leading his horses into the clearing. The young man stepped toward him with hand extended. "I'm Gabriel Laurent."

Wolf gripped his hand. "Oliver Wolf."

"And the young lady with the shotgun is my sister, Margo."

Margo nodded, but her lips were pressed tight and her eyes were not welcoming.

Gabriel gestured toward the pregnant woman, who seemed unsteady on her feet and did not look well. "This is...is Angelina Laurent."

"My pleasure, ma'am." Wolf noted the hesitation in Gabriel's introduction and thought it a bit strange given that they all shared a last name.

Margo moved to Angelina's side and helped ease her onto a blanket so she could sit.

Gabriel asked, "Are you the man who was firing the rifle from the other side of the canyon?"

"I am. You were about to have company. And they weren't acting like folks you wanted to see."

"How many?"

"Two. One was a big man."

"That would have been Beast. The other was likely Hugo."

"So, you do know the men?"

"Yes. They are part of a gang that has taken over the Bar P. We are trying to escape and get to Santa Fe. My father, Adam Laurent, and Angelina own the Bar P."

"I know the place. The Perez land grant. Where is your father?"

"He is being held at the ranch by the gang. His life is in danger. Angelina was going to be killed. My father asked me to take her to Santa Fe. We must see a doctor, the U. S. Marshal, and a lawyer in that order."

"What gang is this? Who is the leader?"

"The leader? My mother. This is all very complicated. I cannot take time to explain now. We must move on to Santa Fe."

"I am heading there myself. I know the trails. I can ride with you, if that is your wish."

Gabriel showed faint traces of a smile and sighed. "Mister Wolf, we would welcome your company."

"Oliver will do. May I speak with Angelina?"

"Of course."

Wolf walked with Gabriel to the blanket where Angelina lay and knelt beside her. "Ma'am, tell me how you are feeling. Are you having contractions? Labor pains? Do you feel like the baby is coming?"

"No. I do not think so. But I do not know about these things. This is my first child. I just hurt. Here." She pressed her abdomen. "And here." She pointed to her thighs. "And here." She rubbed her back. "But mostly, I just want to sleep."

Wolf had assisted with the birth of several human babies on the Cherokee reservation and a good number of foals and occasional calves. He figured the process for all creatures was about the same. He was not all that intimidated by the prospects of a human baby's birthing but preferred to let his friend, Dr. Micah Rand, preside over the process in Santa Fe. He guessed the woman was more exhausted than anything. Certainly she was in no condition to make a mountain trek by horseback. Wolf looked up at Gabriel. "We need to make camp here and stay the night. She needs rest, and so do your horses. How long have you been on the trail?"

"We left the ranch in the middle of the night the night before last. We haven't stopped to sleep, only to rest a spell now and then—maybe nap an hour—and to eat. Our food supplies ran out the first day out. We just grabbed a half loaf of bread, a can of beans, and a jar of canned apples on our way out."

"We've got to get you fed. I've got supplies on the packhorse. You get a fire started. I've got beans and bacon, and I'll bake some biscuits. After we eat, you and I will construct a travois for Angelina."

"A travois?"

"It's sort of a bed that drags behind the horse. Not like sleeping on a feather mattress, but she can sleep on it while we travel, and it will be a lot easier on her than straddling a horse in her condition."

"How long to Santa Fe?" Gabriel asked.

"We'll be moving like snails, so we should head east. It will be smoother going. We'll cross the Rio Grande near Taos, well before the Chama meets up with it. A little longer but easier on Missus Laurent. It will take us most of two days to get to Taos, where I can probably rent a wagon and team. After that, it's at least two, and more likely three days at our pace, to Santa Fe. We can pick up more food supplies in Taos."

"Won't Beast and Hugo catch up with us?"

"They could if they turn around and head back this way. I'll ride back up the trail after dark and see if there is any sign of them. I'll ride rear guard till we get to Santa Fe."

Margo Laurent had remained silent throughout the conversation. From her glare, it was obvious she did not trust him. She probably did not like him showing up and taking charge. With her parents at war, perhaps trust did not come easy for her. That was not necessarily a bad thing at her age. As for his taking charge, she had better get used to it. If he was going to stick his nose into some family war, they were going to do things his way, or he was getting the hell out.

Chapter 8

LILITH WAS CONSUMED with rage when Beast and Hugo rode in and reported that the mission to recover her younger children and Adam's whore had been thwarted by a mystery rifleman. She stood on the veranda with Jack at her side, looking down at the pathetic excuses for gunmen who stood embarrassed and crestfallen at the bottom of the steps. "You stupid, cowardly bastards. You couldn't corral two kids and a pregnant pig and bring them back here. I shouldn't pay you a damned nickel for this job."

Beast whined, "Weren't our fault some guy with a buffalo gun showed up. We was closing in and just about had the woman and kids trapped when that feller started pouring lead our way. Couldn't see him, but if we hadn't turned back, he'd have taken us down."

Hugo spoke, his voice more controlled and less defensive. "You ain't paying us enough to die, Miss La Croix. I'll use my gun, and it don't bother me none to kill a man that needs killing, but I ain't going to do suicide. I don't understand what any of this is all about, and it ain't my business so long as I get paid. I don't like this talk about not paying up, so maybe I'll just ride on out."

At least Hugo had some backbone, she thought. The new crew should be riding in anytime, but she didn't know how many were competent with a gun or would use one if ordered. Jack, of course, was worth three men, but Pedro and Raphael were several days away from being any help and had already failed their first tests. Put down by milksoppy Gabriel of all people. Or did her second son have more grit than she had judged? Anyway, she needed the two standing below her—for now. "No. Stay on. You'll have a chance to make up for this. I'll give you each five gold double eagles up front. Jack will give you the money before the day is out. Put up your horses and get some rest."

"What about your husband?" Beast asked. "Is he still in the bunkhouse?"

"No. We've got him tied up in the late cook's room. The bunkhouse will be for you men and the new crew. It's about four o'clock. Supper's at seven in the house. We'll open the ranch cookhouse when the crew shows up."

"But the cook's dead. Are you cooking?" Beast asked.

She responded with an incredulous look. "Hell no, you simpleton. Pedro's chief cook, and Raphael is his assistant until we come up with something better. I hope you like burnt tamales. Now, please go. I've got work to do."

She was still angry with Pedro for cutting the cook's throat. It had caused a terrible inconvenience. His punishment had been the cook assignment. Since he was now blind in one eye and the other was swollen half shut, she had drafted Raphael to assist, meting out retribution for his own stupidity for being outsmarted by his brother. Raphael was himself coping with dizziness, stumbling around like a saloon drunk. The two of them didn't make a man right now, and she had never eaten slop like they put together. She was willing to pay a nice bonus to any cowhand with even mediocre cooking skills who showed up with the new crew.

"What are we going to do about Adam?" Jack asked.

"We are going to see that he makes out a will."

"A will?"

"Yes, a document that leaves all his property to his beloved wife, Lilith La Croix. In his own handwriting.

Pierre, our New Orleans lawyer, told me that such a will does not require witnesses. He called it holographic, as I recall. We do not want witnesses." She did not add that she had procured this information during a nightlong frolic in the young lawyer's bed, although Jack would not have been surprised to hear it. She would rendezvous with him again when she returned to New Orleans. He was an excellent lawyer and a very proficient lover, not as good as Jack, perhaps, but offering a welcome change in techniques, which she sometimes craved.

"You don't really think he would do that?"

"With a bit of persuasion."

"But even if he signs a will, he can change it the next day."

"Not if he is dead."

"You can't just shoot him. That would raise more questions. You cannot inherit his property with a hangman's noose around your neck."

"He will enjoy a public death, so that many will see that we did not inflict it. To all witnesses it will appear he died of natural causes. None will be aware that he met his end by an undetectable poison created by my good friend, Mambo Lucia, from mandrake roots. He may hallucinate a bit and vomit some before his throat begins to swell and he suffocates—not a pleasant death, Mambo assured me. I have witnessed the results on some of my business competitors. Very effective. No one was the wiser."

"You never told me about that. But I know you have visited Mambo often and paid her well."

"I tell you only what you need to know. It is for your protection sometimes. Now, I must visit with Adam alone. I will need you tonight, so let us retire early. After you have satisfied me, we will talk further of our plans for Adam."

Yes, she and Mambo, the tiny, wizened black woman of French and Haitian descent, were frequent allies. Mambo Lucia had heard the stories of the original Lilith, who was the first Adam's wife before the wicked Eve stole him away. But the Adam of Genesis and Lilith had reproduced first, and their line survived to this day. Mambo had assured her. According to Mambo, the line prospered as a colony of Wulvers—half man and half wolf—in Scotland, and there were other such groups throughout the world. These creatures had the ability to change from human to wolf form and back again at will. And Mambo believed that such potential resided in Lilith, and together they searched for the key that would unlock the secret of this transformation.

Lilith wondered what it would be like to mate with a Wulver or to bear a Wulver's child. Would such offspring be called a baby or a pup? Well, her child-bearing years were nearly ended but not her lust. And for many years, Mambo Lucia had provided a powder, which, if taken after the first missed monthly, assured there would be no child. She thought now of her progeny. Two were hopeless, she finally admitted to herself. Raphael might still be worthy of carrying on her line. Adam had been her mistake. She had been young and foolish and caught up in a fantasy. Jack should have sired all her children. They might even have procreated a Wulver together. Of course, she had not told Jack about Wulvers. He might question her sanity.

Chapter 9

WOLF THOUGHT ANGELINA Laurent's condition had improved considerably after he rented the team and buckboard in Taos and fashioned a reasonably comfortable nest in the wagon bed. They were moving more slowly than he liked because of the rutted Taos road and out of consideration for Angelina's fragile condition. They should reach Santa Fe in a few hours, which would take them to mid-afternoon. What then? It seemed that he had quickly become the decisionmaker for the party, and it was not a welcome task. But he did not have time for democracy, and, if this ragtag outfit did not like his decisions, he would willingly relinquish command.

He liked the young man, Gabriel. He was quick to step in and help with any task and was a quick learner—obviously an educated lad. Angelina was pleasant enough but said little, appearing dazed and confused at times. From the pieces of the story that had leaked out over the days they had been together, he figured she had reason to feel overwhelmed. Margo was a tough kid and carried her share of responsibilities but rarely spoke directly to Wolf, choosing to express any concerns via her brother. She was on the sullen side and clearly did not trust the man she still looked upon as a stranger.

Wolf decided he would drop Angelina and Margo off at Micah Rand's office first. Micha could examine the pregnant woman while he and Gabe reported to Marshal Chance Calder. The lawyers could wait till tomorrow. He would send these folks to Rivers and Sinclair. Danna Sinclair knew more about land grant law than any law wrangler in the territory.

Wolf's neighbors, Josh Rivers, and his wife, Jael Chernik Rivers, were both lawyers with the firm. After several years of residing more than half of each year at Fort Sill in Indian Territory, where Jael had handled Comanche Chief Quanah Parker's personal and business legal matters, the couple would now be working permanently in the Santa Fe office. Wolf was uncertain what legal problems had to be sorted out for the Laurent clan, but Rivers and Sinclair would have the resources to help.

Now, where was he going to put these people for the night? The only decent lodging was offered by the Exchange Hotel. Wolf doubted if the Exchange would have two rooms available this late in the day, and he could not think of anyplace else fit for ladies. Their accommodations should not be his concern. He sighed. But it was not that easy. He had two spare bedrooms in his new home in the foothills a few miles outside of Santa Fe. He did not think his friend and lover, Tabitha Rivers, would object. She knew what it was like to have one's life in crisis. Yes, he would offer these sad strays lodging at his home, but they would take supper at the Exchange before they rode out. He was ready for a good meal that he did not have to prepare, and their cook and housekeeper had been granted a vacation with pay during his absence.

As they neared the outskirts of Santa Fe, he announced his plans. "Angelina, I will introduce you to Dr. Rand, and he will see to any medical needs. Margo, you may stay with her and take note of any medical instructions. Gabe and I will visit the marshal's office. When we have reported to the marshal, we will return here, and then we will all dine at the Exchange Hotel. After that, I will take you to my home northwest of town, and you may stay there for as long as you need."

Margo spoke, "What if we do not wish to stay there?"

"Then I will leave you at the Exchange, and you may do whatever you wish. Your problems will no longer be my concern."

Angelina said with a firmness that surprised him. "Enough, Margo. No more of your rudeness to this kind man who has been our Good Samaritan. Thank you, Oliver, we would be grateful for your hospitality."

"Yes," Gabriel said. "We cannot thank you enough."

"Sorry," Margo said softly but contritely. "Thank you."

Peace made, when they arrived at Dr. Rand's clinic, Wolf and Gabriel assisted Angelina into the doctor's office. There was nothing fancy about the former bootmaker's shop, but Rand, a Quaker and former Army physician just shy of his thirtieth birthday, was building a thriving medical practice. He had recently expanded into an adjacent building and could claim a reception area, examination room, a surgery and a large room with three hospital beds. He even possessed a wood panel on wheels fashioned by Wolf that allowed for separation of the beds by sex.

Rand was occupied with a patient, but the nurse-receptionist, a congenial middle-aged Mexican woman, assured the visitors that he would be able to see Angelina within a half hour. Wolf and Gabriel made a quick exit from the clinic and, leaving the wagon and other horses in front of the doctor's clinic, led their own mounts down the street to the Federal Courthouse, where the marshal's office was located at a side entrance on the ground floor.

They tied their horses to a hitching rail and strolled to the door, which they found locked. A note was tacked to the door frame. Wolf read aloud, "Gone till Sunday. If emergency inquire with office of Territory Gov. Lew Wallace. Chance Calder, U. S. Marshal."

Gabriel said, "Marshal's gone. This is Wednesday. That's four days till he returns. This is an emergency. Where do we find the governor's office?"

"Down the street. We can stop there." He figured the young man should learn for himself about the hopelessness of seeking help from government bureaucrats. It would be worse than hammering your head against an adobe wall. A clerk would have forms to complete. Gabriel would be required write out his grievance. Three or four administrators would consider the matter, and, after two weeks, if Gabriel was lucky, it might reach the governor's desk. The governor might or might not be willing to appoint an acting U. S. Marshal, but it would make no difference because long before that Chance Calder would have returned. The governor was a decent man, Wolf thought, but he was a political appointee and had been in office only a few months since his appointment by President Rutherford B. Hayes earlier in the year. He was likely to avoid making any decision that was not forced upon him by political pressure.

The visit to the governor's office went pretty much as Wolf had scripted in his mind. He had been impressed, however, with Gabriel's competency in handling the paperwork that was thrown at him. He was obviously an intelligent and well-educated young man.

As they led their horses back to the doctor's office, Gabriel said, "We wasted our time there, didn't we?"

"Maybe. But I've got a thought." He turned and headed toward The Plaza.

Gabriel followed but said nothing. They arrived at an office with a sign above the door. White with black antique lettering, the sign read "Rivers and Sinclair" in large print on one line and below that in smaller letters, "Lawyers."

"Wait here," Wolf said, handing Owl's reins to Gabriel. "I'll be back in a few minutes."

When Wolf returned, Gabriel looked at him questioningly. Wolf said, "We've got an appointment with Danna Sinclair in the morning. She will see us at ten o'clock tomorrow. Angelina can get advice on her legal problems, but we might get some other help as well. It so happens that Danna is one of the town's leading Republicans,

President Hayes' and Governor Wallace's party. Women may not have the vote, but Danna's got a silver tongue and is Santa Fe's leading suffragist. Politicians ignore her at their peril. She might be willing to intercede on your behalf."

"I hope so. Something's got to be done. Soon."

Chapter 10

STARLIGHT CAST A soft glow on the mesa when Wolf and his party approached the two ranch homes that were separated by less than fifty yards. He was not surprised to see lamplight sifting through the curtains of the Josh and Jael Rivers renovated adobe house as they passed, but he had not expected to find his new home and studio swallowed by total blackness. Where was Tabby?

Then he noticed a glimmer of light dancing like a firefly from inside the stable behind the house. Perhaps she was checking on the horses. Odd, though, that she had not left a lamp on in the house. He signaled the riders to rein in near the wide wrap-around veranda. They unloaded the gear and supplies on the porch, and then Wolf led them into the front room of the residence.

He lighted a large kerosene lamp just inside the doorway to reveal a modest-sized room with oak floors partially covered by several buffalo hide rugs and furnished with a stuffed leather settee and assorted matching chairs. Rustic tables of various sizes, precisely crafted by Wolf, were within easy reach of every chair. Lamps were placed on two for reading comfort. The smooth pine walls were covered with Wolf's favorite paintings, some awaiting sale, but the room was dominated by a huge fireplace recessed into a wall of precisely carved rose-colored granite stones of differing shapes and sizes that constituted an artwork of its own.

"Be seated ladies," he said. "I will get a fire started to remove the chill, and then Gabe and I will put up the horses. Tabby appears to be in the stable. I will tell her we have guests, and I assure you she will be delighted to welcome you." The reality was that Tabby would feign delight but would chide him about bringing home strays again. It was not that she was opposed to helping someone coping with troubles, but she preferred a bit of notice. He was confident, however, that when she heard of the Laurent dilemma, she would leap into the fray, likely seeking out a story to write for the *Santa Fe Daily New Mexican*.

After a crackling fire began to toss some heat into the cozy room, Wolf and Gabriel led the horses to the stable. There was ample space because the frame structure offered fifteen stalls. Wolf's small herd consisted of five pregnant mares currently carrying foals sired by Owl. He had constructed the large stable with an eye to the future. He owned five hundred acres of some of the best grass in New Mexico, acquired when he and the neighboring Rivers couple had split a thousand-acre parcel they had purchased together. His ranch was miniscule by New Mexican standards, but he sometimes could not believe the good fortune that had come his way since his arrival in Santa Fe almost four years earlier. Of course, he carried a hefty mortgage at the Spiegelberg brothers' Second National Bank, but, if his art and construction enterprises continued to prosper, he would have that paid in three or four years.

When they led the horses through the open stable door, Wolf was surprised to find the human occupant was not Tabitha Rivers. A tall sable-haired young woman with lightly bronzed skin, reflecting Spanish heritage on her mother's side, stood next to one of the stalls with pitchfork grasped in her hands. "Hi, Oliver," Rylee O'Brian said, offering a broad smile and looking questioningly at Gabriel.

"Rylee? I didn't expect to find you here."

"Tabby asked me to look after the horses. I let them out to graze during the day, but she wanted them put up in the stable at night. I was late getting home from work so I didn't get them grained and cared for till after dark. And I have to take time to dote on them a bit."

"I appreciate that. But I know it's an imposition."

"Not at all. I love horses. Besides, Tabby overpaid me to do this."

Eighteen-year-old Rylee managed bookkeeping and carried a vice-president's title at the Spiegelberg brothers' Second National Bank of Santa Fe. She was a budding young capitalist with an aptitude for numbers and money management. She appeared clueless about her own dark beauty and how she affected local males. As far as Wolf knew, the young woman was more interested in banking than any of the cowboys who trailed her like puppies and vied for a smile or a nod. "Where's Tabby? How long have you been doing chores?"

"I don't know where she went. Jael said she left a note for you. I've been looking after the horses for a week now. She's already paid me for another week, so if you have other business, I can keep doing chores for as long as you need me. Let me take care of the horses you've got there." Her gaze fixed on Gabriel. "You didn't introduce us."

"Oh, sorry. Rylee, this is my friend, Gabriel Laurent. He and his sister and stepmother are my guests for a few days. Gabe, meet Rylee O'Brian. She's part of the Rivers family, my neighbors. When she's not cleaning stables, she works at the Second National Bank."

Gabriel removed his hat, his eyes not averting Rylee's obvious perusal of him. "My pleasure, ma'am."

Wolf did not have time to waste while the two young people appraised each other like a pair of wary cats. He wanted to locate Tabitha's note to find out what the hell was going on.

Gabriel intervened and freed him to return to the house. "Oliver, why don't you head back to the house? I can take care of the horses and help Miss O'Brian finish up here."

"Is that okay with you, Rylee?" Wolf asked.

"It doesn't matter, but I suppose it would help to have two putting up all these horses."

"Very well. I will leave the horses for the two of you to take care of. I'll go see if I can start getting folks settled in at the house." When he departed the stable, the silence between Gabriel and Rylee snapped quickly, and he could already hear the young woman barking out instructions. She was a bossy sort, and it would be interesting to see how things played out between them.

He found Angelina asleep on the settee in front of the fireplace when he entered the house. Margo came into the front room from the adjacent hallway. "I hope it is okay," she said, "I have given myself a tour of your home. I just peeked in the doorways. I promise I didn't touch anything."

"That's quite all right. Saves me the trouble of showing you around."

"You have a studio that would be the envy of every artist in New Orleans. You were not kidding. You truly are an artist, aren't you?"

"I am trying to be."

"Do you write, also? I saw the office with the Remington typewriter and stacks of paper on the desk and side table."

"No, Tabby's the writer. Tabitha Rivers. She's my . . . my . . ."

Margo smiled and said, "You don't need to explain. I'm from New Orleans."

Wolf shrugged and grinned sheepishly. "Anyway, she's far more successful in her field than I am in mine. She is quite well known for her novel, *The Last Hunt* and a non-fiction work, *Dismal Trail*. Both books are about the last days of the Comanche before they went to the reservation. She is an independent writer now but does special assignments for the *Daily New Mexican*."

"I love novels. I will have to find and purchase a copy. Do you think she would sign it for me?"

"I'm sure she would be delighted. I suspect there are extra publisher's copies in her office. I'll see if I can find you one after we get you and Angelina settled for the night."

"Oh, that would be wonderful. How can you be so nice to me? I've been such a bitch."

Wolf smiled, "I wouldn't put it that harshly. But I do understand, though, that you are dealing with a very difficult situation in your family. I can't blame you for being on edge and a little suspicious."

"What about Miss Rivers? Was she in the stable? Will she be here soon?"

"No. Tabby has taken a trip someplace, I guess. That was a young neighbor lady who is looking after the horses. Gabe and she are putting up our mounts, and he is going to help her finish chores."

"I hope she's ugly and unpleasant. Gabe's always been a lone wolf and has his nose in books all the time. I don't think he knows much about women, and I don't want some hussy to break his heart. He wanted to be a professor or doctor or lawyer. Mother didn't think such things were manly pursuits."

"Well, I don't think anybody would call Rylee O'Brian ugly, but I doubt if she's any danger to your brother." He did not add that he figured any woman had lethal potential to a vulnerable man under the right circumstances. He had figured he was inoculated against love after two tragic endings, but he had not accounted for a woman like Tabby Rivers taking his heart.

Margo insisted she and Angelina would share a room and bed, and she wakened the expectant mother and led her into one of the spare bedrooms. "I want to keep an eye on her," she explained. "Dr. Rand thinks it will be another month, but the strain she's under could cause the baby to come early", he said.

The fifteen-year-old girl was showing remarkable maturity, Wolf thought, and was assuming serious responsibility for a stepmother, who was easily young enough to be the girl's older sister. He supposed it was understandable if this Lilith was as evil as some of the comments he had overheard, which he doubted.

Margo held him to his promise to find a copy of *The Last Hunt* and then joined Angelina in bed, starting the book under dim lamplight. Wolf went to the bedroom he shared with Tabitha and found her note in an envelope on top of their bed. He picked it up and took it to the front room and, after adding a few logs to the fire, sat down in a chair adjacent to a lamp table, opened the envelope and slipped out the sheet of parchment. The letter was written in her own hand, one reason that the typewriter was her indispensable writing tool, Wolf had occasionally teased. With some trepidation and shaky hands, he held the letter in front of him and read:

Dear Oliver:

This is a coward's letter. I simply could not bring myself to discuss with you the things I have been thinking of late. It is time for us to separate for a spell, perhaps, a long time, perhaps forever. I have left all my belongings, except my travel needs, in the house. You may do as you see fit with them. Someday, I hope to return to see if they are still there, and we can discuss then if we have any future together.

I do not expect you to wait for me. You should probably find another who can give you the life you deserve. I have come to realize I am a nomad and will likely always feel the call of an unbroken trail that might yield my next book or story.

I am going to Taos to talk to my Aunt Dezba at the Pueblo village. My brother Cal will meet me there and will travel with me to the land of the Navajo, where I hope to learn of my ancestors. As you know, I also have an abiding interest in the Apache and their culture, so I expect to journey to Fort Defiance to the south to see what connections I might make from there.

I will be visiting places where posting letters may be difficult and infrequent, but I will try to let you know where I am and what I am doing when I can.

I am wronging you. I cannot rationalize that I have been fair to you. But know this: I have never lied when I said, "I love you." Never. I do love you, and I shall never love another as I do you. I hate the thought of you being with another woman, but you are free with my blessing. I do not expect you to wait, and I am not entitled to your misplaced fidelity.

Other than Cal, Jael is the only person to whom I have spoken about my plans. Except for you, she is my dearest friend, and she will be there for you, if you will let her.

Please do not think of me with too much loathing for what I have done to you.

Love always,

Tabby

Wolf rested the letter on his lap and stared into the fire, tears stinging his eyes, the first since he returned from the War of the Rebellion and learned that the woman he loved had married his twin brother and borne his twin's child, shattering the dreams he had clung to during the dark years of his absence. His mind raced. Should he follow her? He could easily track her down. But then what? Shouldn't they at least talk about this crazy plan of hers?

His thoughts were interrupted when the front door opened, and Gabriel entered with a beaming face. "Took you a spell," Wolf observed.

"Yeah. Rylee and I talked some. She's a fascinating lady. She is going to help me open an account at the bank tomorrow. She said she would have dinner with me at The Exchange at noon so long as I was paying. Well, of course. Why wouldn't I?"

It was already too late. Wolf knew better than anybody. The kid was taking his first step on the road to hell.

Chapter 11

DANNA SINCLAIR, JOSH Rivers and Jael Chernik Rivers were gathered about the table in the Sinclair and Rivers conference room discussing planned changes in the firm's organization. Danna, although junior in seniority to Josh in the law firm he had founded, led the discussion because she acted as managing partner. Josh had neither temperament nor interest in handling day to day business affairs and recognized that the firm had started generating serious revenues only after Danna joined the practice.

"So, you are both still comfortable with the decision? You will settle permanently in Santa Fe and work out of this office? And Marty Locke will move to the Fort Sill office with Tara after their wedding next month?"

Josh replied, "I don't see another alternative. This office obviously produces triple the legal work. Even though

Quanah Parker and the reservation tribes provide serious revenues, one lawyer can handle routine tribal work. Jael can travel to Indian Territory several times a year to meet personally with Quanah and the other chiefs. And Quanah increasingly has Santa Fe investments for her to attend to. Now that Jael has been admitted to the bar, the firm can't afford to maintain two lawyers at Sill."

Jael, formerly known as She Who Speaks, spoke fluent Comanche as well as four other languages and was the firm's critical link to Quanah. She had been a Comanche captive born of a slain Jewish couple, but her affinity for languages and quick intelligence had blazed a trail that led her to a position as counselor to the Comanche war chief. This had been unprecedented for a woman among the Comanche. She and her Comanche husband had also adopted a captive toddler who happened to be Josh Rivers's son, Michael. A subsequently widowed She Who Speaks, through a bizarre chain of events, had ultimately encountered and married the boy's natural father. Upon Quanah's surrender and relocation on the Fort Sill reservation, she had read the law as a clerk in the firm and recently passed the examination for admission to the territorial bar.

Jael said, "It is decided. I will return to the reservation whenever Quanah summons me, but Marty will gain

Quanah's confidence. Besides, the work for the Comanche will involve increasing litigation, and there is no better trial lawyer than Marty. And Tara Cahill will be a perfect clerical assistant. I look for our secretary, Rabbit, to eventually leave the reservation, but she should be in the office for another year to act as interpreter and, perhaps, help them learn some of the Comanche language."

Danna said, "I think you will do well here with your fluency in Spanish. Josh says you are quickly learning to read the language as well. That will prove invaluable."

"I hope so. I should be able to refine my reading and writing skills if we are living and working full-time in Santa Fe. But I hope to spend much of my time on Indian affairs if I can gain some reputation in that area. I have been assured that the Kiowa tribe's council will approve retaining our firm at its next meeting. We should be aware that all the tribes are beginning to recognize the need for legal counsel in negotiating treaties and guiding them through the maze of changes in Indian policies. An agreement made today is only valid if the next president or congress chooses to honor its terms. Someone must chart the course for addressing these grievances. We can perform valuable services for the tribes and do good—and earn a decent living while doing so."

Danna tossed a glance at the Regulator clock on the wall. "I have an appointment in ten minutes. Oliver Wolf set it up for some folks named Laurent. It sounds like a French name. Do either of you know these people?"

"Not me," Josh said.

Jael said, "Rylee mentioned a young man with that name—Gabriel, as I recall—when she came in from doing chores at Oliver's last night. She was vague about the relationships. Gabriel had a sister with the group, and he referred to another woman as his father's wife—not stepmother. Rylee said he avoided talking about how they came to know Oliver. But I can tell you she was quite taken with the young man. She babbled on about how intelligent and handsome he was. I must say this is the first I have ever seen her much enthused about a male of the species."

"It's about time," Danna said. "Good grief. She turned eighteen a few weeks ago."

"She has always been so absorbed in her fascination with business. And she worships Willi Spiegelberg, who is old enough to be her grandfather."

"Willi adores her, too." Danna said. "But it is her mind that fascinates him, and his wife is willing to tolerate that type of adoration."

"Speaking of Wolf," Jael said, "I suspect he is going to want to talk to me about Tabby. Rylee said she told him last night, and Tabby said she was leaving a letter, which he would have found by now. I feel so badly for him. Tabby is my friend and sister-in-law, but I am a bit miffed at her treatment of him. She should have spoken to him face to face."

Josh interjected, "She was afraid he would talk her out of the craziness, which I cannot come near to understanding. But Tabby has always had that wild streak that led her off on one quest or another. That's how she ended up spending the winter in a Comanche village with a crazy Indian woman called She Who Speaks."

Jael just rolled her eyes.

Chapter 12

DANNA HAD NO difficulty identifying the members of the Laurent family when she entered her private office. Her secretary, Linda de la Cruz, had moved an additional chair into the room, and the three family members and Wolf were already seated in front of her desk. The pregnant woman stuffed in a snug dress, which Danna recognized as Tabby's, was obviously the wife of the father of the young lady and man who accompanied her. She was a tiny woman, so by casting aside petticoat and puffy undergarments, she had been able to squeeze into Tabby's dress. Tabitha was slender and willowy but probably nearly a half foot taller than the wearer of her garment, who might reach five feet in heels thicker than the non-existent ones on the sandals she wore.

Danna introduced herself, and the visitors stood and shook hands with her before sitting again. The sun shone brightly and streamed through the window, casting its glow on Danna and turning her long, strawberry-blonde hair to spun gold. She set pencil and paper aside, knowing that a lawyer's note taking sometimes made a client uneasy and inhibited conversation. She had nearly perfect recall and would do her writing after the clients departed. "What can I help you with?" Danna asked, addressing the group until she identified the spokesperson.

The young man with dark, seductive eyes replied. It was no surprise Rylee was taken with him, she thought. "We have a family problem that is very complicated to sort out. Worst of all, we believe my father's life is in danger. We owe our own lives to Oliver, and we asked him to join us here. You may speak freely in his presence."

Bright young man, clearing up any confidentiality issues immediately. "Perhaps you had better start from the beginning."

"I only know part of the story, but I will tell you what I am aware of. We are from New Orleans, a place of many cultures and races that have intermingled for several centuries. Religions and beliefs are also numerous, and many residents have absorbed a mixture of faiths, a religion for each occasion, if you will. You must first understand that my mother's mind is not right. She is very intelligent, frighteningly so, but she has very strange ideas and is utterly without conscience. Her name is Lilith. She claims to be a descendent of Adam's first wife, whose name was Lilith."

"Adam? You mean the Adam from the Bible? In Genesis?"

"Yes."

"I am not a Biblical scholar, but I have never heard of such a person."

"Most people have not. I think it is a story from a Jewish legend. I don't know much about it. My mother got the idea from her father. He was a mulatto and free Negro, who married a woman of Spanish and Cherokee descent. He called himself a Christian but was also a believer in the practices of the voodoo mambos. I don't know where he picked up the notion he was descended from Adam and Lilith, and I don't know much about the legend. But when my mother met my father, whose name is Adam, she took it as a sign that they were meant to be married. Father would have had no chance when she set her sights on him."

"My head is spinning. Just tell me how everyone ended up in New Mexico Territory."

Margo spoke. "My mother was very cruel and determined I should be like her. She said she would train me to wear the crown of Lilith and that someday I might even be a wolf creature. It was very scary. I was often disobedient, and she took her whip to me when she was angry. I have the scars on my back to prove it. She even spoke of mating me with my brother, Raphael, to increase the concentration of the Lilith line. I told my father, and he promised that would never happen and that she would not beat me. A few days later, we departed for Santa Fe. We both spoke Spanish as well as French and English, and, with our dark coloring, he believed we could 'melt in' here as he put it. He underestimated Mother."

Gabriel explained how his mother had hired the Pinkerton Agency to locate his father and sister and told of the trek to the Bar P ranch and the assault launched there by Lilith and her hired guns. "A man named Pedro raped and murdered the cook. I did not see the bodies, but I heard the guns and I saw the blood when I visited the bunkhouse where they were holding my father. I am certain all the cowhands on the ranch were killed. I do not know what she has in mind, but my mother is convinced she will own the ranch, which she claims is in Father's name."

Danna was incredulous. During her fledgling career, she had heard many strange tales, but she thought it would likely require passage of many years to rival this one. "So you decided to escape?"

"It was at Father's urging. He insisted Mother would kill Angelina and the child she carries. And I could not be a part of what Mother was doing there. I promised Father I would try, but if we had not encountered Oliver, we would not be here today. I fear for my father's life, though."

"Have you contacted the United States Marshal?"

"Yes," Oliver said, "but he is out of town and will not return for some days yet. Gabriel completed the forms at the Governor's office requesting appointment of an acting marshal, but you know how fast that works. I was hoping you might intercede."

Danna pondered Wolf's remark. She had doused more than one political fire for Governor Lew Wallace. She had no doubt she could gain immediate entrance to his office and have Gabriel's request placed at the top of the paper pile. "Are you willing to accept appointment as acting marshal, Oliver?"

"Me? Well, I don't know about that."

"You have served as Chance Calder's special deputy on many occasions, and you already know what this is about. I need to take a recommendation to the governor if I am going to approach him."

Wolf sighed and fidgeted in his chair. Danna had him cornered, and she knew it. He hesitated for a few moments before he replied. "I'll do it. Reluctantly. But be sure I have authority to deputize. This is more than a one-man job."

"I will see the governor first thing after this noon's dinner. But he will not be in until two o'clock. He religiously naps after dining. But you can start looking for deputies. They will have to file claims for their services."

"And get paid in six months if they're lucky," Wolf added.

"I can get an acting marshal appointed, but I cannot expedite payment of claims against the government. That's one reason our firm declines government work. Now we need to discuss other matters." She turned to Angelina. "If I understand correctly, you are the heiress to the Perez land grant?"

"Yes, it has been held by my family for many generations. But I am the first woman to hold the grant. All others have been male descendants. My father had no sons."

"But the land is titled in your husband's name. Why?"

"The grant was being challenged by men in the Santa Fe League. They claimed that the terms of the grant provided that the land could not be held by a woman. They offered to buy the land at one-fourth of its value and take the risk of defending the title. Adam said they were trying to steal the land. He suggested I transfer the title to his name. Then title would be held by a man and would be more difficult to challenge."

Danna did not say so, but she found the whole plan preposterous. A significant portion of her law practice dealt with land grant defense. The early grants originated from the sovereign King of Spain when the Spaniards initially occupied the vast lands now constituting the New Mexico Territory. After Spain ceded its rights to Mexico, that country recognized the validity of the Spanish grants but commenced its own grant system for those lands not previously claimed. When Mexico surrendered the territory to the United States, the successor country continued to recognize most of the grants until divested by court decisions entered because of fraud, grant violations or other flaws concocted by lawyers and placed before the judges. "Did you confer with a lawyer when you made this transfer?"

"No. We just went to the land office, and I signed the papers."

Danna withheld judgment for the moment on whether Adam Laurent was hopelessly naïve or a crook. There was the old saying, of course, that a man who represented himself had a fool for a lawyer. "Tell me about your marriage to Adam. Did you know he had been married previously?"

"Yes, of course. He and Margo showed up one day at the ranch. Adam said he was a ranch manager and heard I might need help. He was a gift from God. My father had died a year earlier, and I knew nothing—and cared nothing—about managing such an operation. I knew my foreman was stealing from me, but I was afraid of the man. Adam took over and fired the foreman. He and Margo moved into the house. But do not misunderstand. We had separate bedrooms. It was all very proper."

"It was," Margo affirmed. "Father was always a gentleman, and he and Angelina were friends for almost a year before they became more to each other. Father and I joined the church during that time."

"Yes. I consider myself devout. I would never have thought of romance with a man who did not share my faith. It was the day after their baptism and confirmation that Adam and Margo shared the story of their escape from Lilith. Not long afterward, we began to speak of our feelings for each other and soon were in love. Adam said he wanted to marry me, but the first wife in New Orleans would find him if he notified her of a divorce, and we were told by a court clerk that notice to

Lilith would be required. We spoke to the priest, and he said that the first marriage was not valid in the eyes of the church and that he could marry us. So we married. It has been almost ten months now. The land was transferred a short time after that."

"I must tell you," Danna said, "that because there was no marriage in the eyes of the church does not mean that there was none in the view of the law."

"I do not care about the law. Only the church is important."

"I respect your religious views, but Lilith Laurent has a potential claim to your land since it is titled in Adam's name. In case of divorce, she could claim half, or in the event of his death, she might inherit all, or at least part."

"Mother uses her maiden name," Gabriel pointed out. "La Croix. Lilith La Croix."

"And I do not care what she calls herself," Angelina said. "She can have the land. I want my husband alive and safe. I wish to employ you to sort out this legal confusion. But the land is nothing without Adam."

Danna thought that Angelina's statement was one she had heard others make about the importance of a loved one, but many faltered when reckoning day came. But something about this young woman suggested she meant it.

Chapter 13

GABRIEL HAD NOTICED Rylee's surprise when he dropped five thousand dollars in gold coinage on the desk of the Second National Bank's sole female employee. When he had told her the previous night that he needed to open a bank account, he was certain she assumed he would be depositing a token amount. She had remained businesslike and matter of fact in setting up his account. But now, as they sat in The Exchange Hotel dining area enjoying plates of steak and fried potatoes, he was convinced the money had caused her to look upon him with increasing curiosity and interest.

He did not judge Rylee a predatory woman seeking a wealthy man, but she appeared to have something of an obsession with finances and commerce and, certainly, an aptitude for management of money. He smiled at his own surprise when he sat down at Rylee's desk and saw the nameplate identifying her as a vice-president of the bank. No, Rylee O'Brian would not require a man's money to help her through life. She was perfectly capable of earning her own.

"This is very good," Rylee said. "Are you going to buy me pie?"

The young woman had an appetite that belied her slim figure. She was half-teasing, he thought, yet she was probably too frugal to buy her own. "Of course. I invited you to dine with me, and that would include dessert. And you now know I can afford it."

She shrugged and smiled, and he could see she was too professional and polite to ask about the source of his funds.

"I wish I could say I earned the money. I did—part of it, doing dock work and whatever I could earn to squirrel away, so I could go away to school and not be dependent on my parents for support—my mother, especially. But when my father left and came out here a few years back, he left a note for me that he had set up an account in the bank for me to provide me a stake, so to speak, when I was ready to go out on my own. He had a friend with the bank who was trustee of the funds, and all I had to do was claim it when I turned eighteen. I waited a year beyond that until my mother announced we were coming west to find Father. That's when I claimed the funds, thinking I might need them here to help Father. Regardless, I knew I would not be returning to New Orleans with Mother."

"My parents are dead, killed by Comancheros. They abducted me and planned to sell me to a bordello in Mexico after they were done with me. But Jael Rivers—she was called She Who Speaks by the Comanche then—rescued me and took me in. I wasn't quite fourteen when it happened. I never talk about it. I don't know why I said anything now."

Gabriel was horrified by the disclosure. His trials with his mother were nothing compared to what Rylee must have faced. "I'm sorry. I had no idea."

"Well, Jael's folks were killed by Comanche and she was taken captive at about the same age I was when my folks were killed. She lived through the initial shock and then made the best of it. She eventually became an important counselor to the Comanche war chief, Quanah. She says we cannot rewrite our histories, but we can learn from them and start a new story whenever we choose."

"That's what I am looking to do. Start a new story. One that doesn't have my mother in it."

"It must be terrible to feel that way about your mother."

"I really haven't thought that much about it. She's the only mother I've ever had. Do you have time to hear a short version of my story?"

Rylee opened the case of the tiny watch that was suspended from a gold chain about her neck. "I do not have to account for my hours at the bank. I always work late, but it seems strange if I don't return by one o'clock. Today, I will make an exception. Tell me."

Gabriel gave Rylee a brief summary of his childhood years but focused on his father's departure with Margo and his mother's quest to locate them. He saw Rylee's eyes widen with disbelief when he told about Lilith's obsession with her belief in her destiny as a descendant of Adam's first wife and her takeover of the Bar P ranch. The expression on her face turned very sad when he told her about his father's imprisonment and request that Gabriel escape with Angelina and Margo.

"You do not really believe your mother would have directed someone to murder Angelina?" Rylee asked.

"No. She would have done it herself. And she will do the same with my father if it serves her purpose to do so. That's why I plan to return to the ranch with Oliver as soon as he swears in some deputies. I hope we can leave yet this afternoon. Oliver says there are shortcuts off travelled wagon trails but it is still at least a two or three-day ride travelling light."

"Do you care if I talk with my employer, Willi Spiegelberg, about the legend of Adam's first wife? He's the bank president, and he and his four brothers own the bank and the largest mercantile in the Southwest. They are Jewish, and Willi is something of a scholar on their heritage. I won't mention names."

"No, not at all. If you promise to dine with me again—as my guest—and tell me what you learned."

"I don't see how I could decline if I am to be your guest. You will find free meals are always an enticement for me. But I take that as a promise that you will be very careful on your mission to the ranch and return safely."

"I promise." He would promise anything to see Rylee O'Brian again.

Chapter 14

WOLF WAS DISCOURAGED when he returned to the Rivers and Sinclair office to report to Danna that he had recruited only a single deputy, Moses Monroe. Mose was a former slave approaching his seventieth year but moved like a man twenty years younger. Only a head of thick snow-white hair betrayed his age. Mose worked as a stableman at The Exchange livery and kept his mouth shut and ears open. Most folks did not even notice his presence, but Wolf had formed a fast friendship with the wily man who had lived a dozen years with the Comanche after running away from a Louisiana plantation.

When Mose had overheard Wolf trying to recruit deputies from men who had no interest in a potential altercation with outlaws or were dubious about a deputy's pay, Mose had stepped up to Wolf and said, "Need something different to do for a spell. I'll ride with you if you can work it out with the boss man. Ain't too busy here lately and the other boys been sitting on their asses playing cards most of the day. Let them pick up some slack while I have me some fun."

Wolf had warned Mose of the possible dangers before clearing his absence with the stable manager, but the old man just shrugged. Wolf had encountered Gabriel outside The Exchange, and the young man confirmed he wanted to ride with the marshal's party to the Bar P. Wolf figured he would deputize him. They agreed to meet at Wolf's house at about three o'clock, which would give him more than another hour to round up a few more deputies. The ladies could make themselves at home at his place during Wolf's and Gabriel's absence. Rylee would care for his horses and check in on the house occupants at least daily.

When he entered the law office and asked to see Danna, Linda de la Cruz waved him on. When he reached Danna's doorway, he saw that Josh Rivers was standing in front of the desk where Danna was seated, attired in a nicely tailored suit of all things. Jael must be trying to dude him up some. He rapped softly on the doorframe. "If you're busy, I can come back later."

"No. Come in, Oliver. It will just be a minute." Danna stood and began shuffling through the clutter on her desk.

"Hello, Oliver," Josh said, "I hear you're going to be a United States Marshal."

"So it appears, but nobody wants to be a deputy. I've got old Moses Monroe and the Laurent kid so far. And that's likely all it's going to be."

"From what I hear, you'd better have more help than that."

"I guess I'm not much of a salesman."

Danna handed Wolf a badge. "Here's a marshal's badge. The governor's clerk found this in an office drawer. Consider yourself sworn." She scooped a handful of badges off the desk. "These are for deputies."

"I won't need that many."

Josh reached over and snatched one of the badges from Danna's hand. He held it up and studied it for a moment. "I think I'd look real good with one of these pinned on, don't you, Oliver?"

Oliver saw the miffed look Danna shot at Josh and subdued a smile. "You would. You surely would."

"I'll ride with you. When are you leaving?"

"I would like to ride out about three o'clock if possible. Mose and Gabriel are supposed to be at my place about that time. I've picked up some food supplies, and the Laurent ladies were going to do some baking today. Can you be ready in that time?"

"Sure. I just need to stop at the house and change into something practical and put my bedroll and other gear together. Chief hasn't had a serious ride since we returned from the reservation a few weeks back, so I'll saddle him up. Does Mose have a decent mount? I can fix him up with one."

"Mose has a string of good horses at his place. He got a Pueblo boy to look after them while he's away. My guess is he will ride his blue roan gelding. Not as strong as your buckskin, but it's a fine animal." Wolf did not add that he doubted either animal was a match for Owl, the stallion he had rescued from the Army's slaughter of over twelve hundred Comanche horses at Palo Duro Canyon.

"Well, I'd better head out to the house," Josh said. "I suppose I'd better step down the hall and tell Jael I won't be home for supper."

Danna said, "You had better ask her to cover your appointments while you are gone. I won't be able to. My schedule's full. That's why we were hoping to have an extra lawyer here with the Fort Sill office trade."

Chapter 15

TABITHA RIVERS HAD spent the better part of a week at the pueblo north of Taos, taking advantage of the wait for her brother Cal's arrival to listen to the stories of the Pueblo people and to learn about their customs and way of life. Ironically, her teacher was full-blood Navajo, or Diné as she sometimes called the tribe of her birth. The word itself in Navajo meant "the People." Dezba was her mother's half-sister, and Tabitha had visited her aunt on two other occasions prior to her current sojourn to the Taos pueblo, the first a year earlier after she had learned that the woman she always believed to be her birth mother, in fact, was not. Tabitha had been a love child born of the affair between her father, Levi Rivers, and Summer Webb, a half-blood Navajo, who at age twenty was nearly twenty-five years younger than her father.

As early evening dropped its dusky blanket over the village, Tabitha sat cross-legged with her aunt in front of a small fire in Dezba's single-room chamber on a second tier of the pueblo. The dancing flames alternately cast a glow, and then shadows, on their faces. She was to meet Cal in Taos in the morning, and she had questions of her aunt before she departed.

Tabitha's fifty-year-old aunt, several years a widow now, was a quiet serene woman, attractive by any standard, and appeared younger than her fifty years. She gazed at Tabitha expectantly, evidently anticipating that her niece wished to talk about something.

"Aunt Dezba, you have told me about my mother's childhood and helped me come to know her. But you have never explained why you and my mother, as Diné, were raised among the Pueblo. I will be travelling to the land of my Diné ancestors, and I would like to know this. Are there relatives there you might wish me to locate?"

Dezba nodded with understanding and spoke softly. "I remember little of the homeland. I was five years old when we came here. Most of what I know I learned from my mother's stories. Her name was Astsam, and my father was called South Wind. During the 1820s and 1830s the Diné were constantly at war with Mexico. Perhaps that is why I was given my name. Dezba means 'war' in the Diné tongue. Shortly after my birth, my father was killed by the Mexican soldiers."

"How did your grandmother meet my grandfather?"

"Your grandfather, Frederick Webb—my stepfather—considered himself a trader, but he was a man of French and English lineage with significant education. He was a cold man at times, seemingly haunted by something in his past. I know he bore some resentment that as a third son he had no claim to inheritance or position in an apparently wealthy family. I believe this is what sent him west. He was strict and demanding but never struck me or harmed me in any way. He spoke English, French, and Spanish fluently and could communicate passably in the languages of the local tribes. I credit him with my learning to speak, read, and write both English and Spanish, which opened the door to my teaching in the missionary schools here and in Taos. I think I have told you that your mother was also fluent in both languages, probably more so than I. She loved to create stories—many about the spirit world—and tell them at a fire in the dark of night."

"Perhaps her storytelling is part of her legacy to me."

"I like to think that. She might have been a writer, but the heart and fate often change the course of lives. Most have 'might have beens' or 'might have dones' in their histories. But I digress. Your grandfather had been commissioned by his cousins, the Bents, a prominent trading family, as you know, to explore the vast Diné lands to determine potential for the fur business and establishment of trading posts there. His exploration was cut short by constant warring between Mexico and the native peoples. But he did meet Astsam there, and your grandparents fell in love. I can assure you he did not take your grandmother as a squaw to share his blanket. I can attest to his devastation when she died on my eighteenth birthday. He was never the same, and though he was in his mid-forties at the time, he never took another wife and died with a broken spirit some ten years later."

"Perhaps that had something to do with his rejection of my mother when he learned of her out-of-wedlock pregnancy."

"Possibly. He had adored your mother. It was he who insisted on changing her name to Summer several years after we arrived in Taos. She was a bright summer sun in his life, he said, and he was raising her for a life in the white world. He did not want her to have an Indian-sounding name, he insisted."

"How did that make you feel?"

"It hurt a bit, but by temperament I do not dwell on such things. Mother taught me to be proud of being Navajo. After all, she was also. The truth is, for no rational reason, she always looked down upon the Pueblo as inferior people. Remember there was a history of conflict between the tribes. However, I am still proudly Navajo, although I have made a nice life among the Pueblo, who have always accepted me as one of theirs. You have met your cousins, my two sons. They are half-blood, but they do not deny their Navajo heritage even as they live among their father's people. North Star even begged as a child for me to teach him the language of the Diné, and he is fluent. Who says we cannot respect and value all of our many parts?"

That was exactly what Tabitha felt. Her latest quest had nothing to do with a rejection of her father's family. She was a Rivers and damned proud of it. But she was called to learn of her Navajo blood. "You had not told me that my mother had a name other than Summer."

"I did not think it important. And I had nearly forgotten. Her birth name was 'Doba,' meaning Peace and was endowed by my mother with hope for a different life for her newborn child. Doba was born in 1834 while my parents were hiding out in a place called the Canyon de Chelly, where Diné had retreated for generations, evading the Spaniards before the Mexicans succeeded to authority and carried on the vendetta. When Summer was barely weaned, there was a brief victory for the Diné when their warriors annihilated a large Mexican patrol at Twin Stars Pass in the Chuska Mountains. But that only brought more Mexican troops, and war promised to be a permanent state."

Tabitha said, "Not a fertile land for peaceful trading it would seem."

"No. My stepfather—your grandfather—decided it would be years before trading efforts would be successful there. He prepared detailed maps of Diné territory, many of which are being used by traders today, but he pulled out and joined Charles Bent in Taos, where he worked for Bent, St. Vrain and Company to develop trade along the Santa Fe Trail. During this time, he set up his own trading post in Taos, where your mother was working when she met your father."

"Do you have relatives among the Navajo people?"

"Cousins, I suppose. My mother said she had two living brothers when we left the nation of the Diné. Her father also lived. They were of the Bear clan, and his name was Tall Pine. I have very dim memories of him. Very tall, hence his name. A man who laughed much. Her brothers were younger and could be alive yet. The youngest, Carries Water, would have been no more than ten years older than I. Runs Fast had two wives. This was unusual, my mother said, because polygamy was not generally practiced among the Diné, but his wives were sisters and, thus, exceptions to the common custom. There was never any contact after we arrived in Taos, so I can tell you nothing more."

"This could be helpful, Aunt Dezba. Thank you for telling me these things. I have had a wonderful visit here with you."

"This has been a time of joy for me. I was there when you were born and took you from your mother's arms that night when she could hold you no more and embarked on her journey to the spirit world. I took you and, grieving as I was for my sister, I thought now I have a daughter. A few weeks later, your father came to claim you, and it broke my heart to let you go. But I have read your books and kept watch on your path through life long before you knew of me, and I am filled with joy and pride at what Summer's child has become. And I know my sister—your mother—is, also."

Chapter 16

TABITHA THOUGHT OF posting a letter to Oliver from Taos, but a stage was passing through daily since the Indian wars in eastern New Mexico had subsided, and she feared he would try to catch up with her if he knew she had recently been in Taos. She assumed he had returned from his trip into the mountains by now and would have read her letter and spoken with Jael. She found she was missing him terribly and starting to question her impulsiveness. She might have saddled up and headed for Santa Fe had Cal not emerged from the boarding house.

When Cal Rivers stepped out onto the boardwalk where she had been waiting, Tabitha was shocked at her brother's appearance. At over six feet and four inches tall, Cal was by far the tallest of the four Rivers brothers, and he had always been a raw-boned, rangy sort, but he appeared haggard and tired, she thought. And his shaggy, straw-colored hair was growing its way to shoulder-length. She hated his brushy moustache but was grateful he was still shaving his cheeks and chin, although he was showing several days stubble. He was attired in a red cotton shirt, buckskin britches, and scuffed boots and had a canvas bag slung over his shoulder and carried a Winchester in his left hand. A Peacemaker revolver was holstered on his waist. Cal had served as a civilian Army scout during the Indian wars and knew how to survive in hostile environments, but he looked terribly fragile today. She wondered if he was fit enough to make the journey she envisioned.

She moved to embrace him, restraining herself for fear she would knock him over.

"Little Sis," he said, hugging her back as best he could with his rifle in hand. "It's been too long."

"Almost a year," she replied. "And you look like a calf with the slobbers. Are you okay? You wrote I should let you know if I was going on an adventure that I needed some company on. But you don't look well. I've got your adventure, but I'm wondering if you are up to it."

Cal nodded toward a bench in front of the adjacent general store. "Let's talk a bit and get our bearings."

She was glad to get him seated someplace before he keeled over. They sat down, and Cal spoke first. "I'll speak a little more kindly of your looks than you did of mine. You look mighty fetching, Little Sis. I always liked you better in buckskins and moccasins. You're just not a dress-wearing, frilly sort. My Lord, I can still see you out there on the old man's Slash R firing that Henry rifle at a row of bottles and putting your older brothers to shame."

"I know I could beat the others, hands down, but I always wondered if you let me win. It seems like you always missed that last bottle." Cal was the youngest of the brothers and five years older than Tabitha and, for some reason, he had always been protective of his little sister.

Cal chuckled. "Maybe someday we'll have us a private shooting match. No quarter."

"I'd like that. Now tell me what's been happening in your life that makes you ripe for adventure. I thought you were busy with that freight hauling partnership with our banker brother." Hamilton Rivers was second eldest of the Rivers brothers and a successful Denver banker. The eldest, Nate, ramrodded the Slash R with their father. Josh, at age thirty-two, was a year older than Cal.

"Well, the partnership is over. We ain't pissed at each other or nothing like that. Ham paid me more than a fair price for my share. But the Atchison, Topeka and Santa

Fe Railway Company will put overland shippers out of business in another five years. The Santa Fe Trail is on its deathbed. The company stole the Santa Fe name, but they won't even have a direct route there. I guess they'll have a spur that connects to the main line. The railroad will be changing the Southwest. It's already happened in Denver, Ham says."

"So are you going back to the ranch?"

"No. That's Erin's. She's made that clear. She's kicked me out anyhow. Won't even let me on the place to see the kids. Of course, I guess I got no legal right to see Willow, beings she was sired by that Comanche warrior when Erin was a captive. But I love that little beauty and think of her as mine. Zack—he's mine, and I don't know if she can legally keep him from me. I can't stand this. My gut hurts all the time. I thought if maybe I went away for a time, my head would clear, and I could figure this out. I ain't saying I don't have some of this shit coming to me."

"You've got lawyers in the family. You need to talk to one of them. I don't see why you would have this treatment coming to you."

Cal sighed. "I been drinking too much. A lot too much. I've said unforgivable things to Erin when I was drinking. Called her a Comanche's whore and worse—not that she didn't hold her own on the name calling. But I did lots of stuff I'm ashamed of."

"You didn't hit her?"

"No, nothing like that. I threw dishes, chopped up her favorite furniture pieces with an axe. That sort of thing. I ain't never hit a woman. Never would no matter how drunk I was."

"I'm glad of that."

"I just got to get away. I got a problem with the liquor. Don't let me near it. Getting the hooch out of my system might be a start."

Two runners, she thought. Cal was running from his problems. She had not figured out what her running was about. "Okay. Let's have a decent breakfast at the restaurant before we head out. I've got Smokey, my gray gelding, at the livery along with a good pack mule. I've collected supplies and gear at the livery, too. We've just got to load the mule. I saw a huge bay gelding in a stall and a bedroll in the runway just outside. I'm betting that's your mount."

"You win your bet. Now tell me where we're travelling."

"I'll tell you at breakfast. You might change your mind yet."

Chapter 17

AS THE FINGERS of dawn's first light crept through the curtains, Lilith stretched and spooned her naked body against Jack's. She loved the sensation of flesh pressing against flesh. She did not know if love was what she felt for Jacques Moreau. She was unsure what love was, but her bond with him was more than that. They were like twin brother and sister sprung from a single seed. Of course, if that were true, their coupling would be taboo. That thought, however, just made her blood run hot again.

She was aware that he had seduced many other women or, more likely, permitted them to seduce him. The thought just made her desire him more. There was no jealousy between them. They each provided an anchor in the other's life, the one person who would fill the void for any need, carnal or otherwise. The trust between them was absolute.

Jack slipped away and rolled over and faced her, meeting her sleepy gaze with those dark probing eyes that removed the need for speech between them. She lowered her eyes and saw that he, of course, was ready, and she started to inch her body toward him and lifted her head to meet his lips. The moment died when she heard yelling and commotion outside the house.

They both rolled out of bed, reaching for their Colts before their garments. They raced to the window, and Lilith pulled the curtain aside just enough to peer out. Riders coming into the yard. Beast and Hugo were waving at the newcomers as if they recognized some of the men. She looked at Jack. "It must be the crew. About time."

They dressed quickly, and, as she passed near the kitchen, Lilith snapped at Pedro, who was standing near the stove looking perplexed. "Get your brown ass moving, mister. We've got guests for breakfast. Rustle Raphael out of bed and tell him I said to help you. He's finished using that knot on his skull as an excuse to loll around."

Jack followed Lilith out onto the veranda. Seven mounted men on horseback, four Anglos and three Mexicans, were bunched together in the yard. Several of the Anglos carried sidearms in holsters slung low on the hip that suggested they thought of themselves as gunslingers. The Mexicans had rifles in their scabbards but had the look of men hungry for honest work. She would have Jack talk to them one on one and see if any might be willing to take up a gun to defend the ranch.

A stocky, thick-shouldered man wearing a leather vest and a grayish low-crowned Stetson hat, caught her eye when he dismounted from his sorrel gelding and handed the reins to a companion. He walked toward the veranda with a cocky strut that she found charming. His eyes fastened on hers and never strayed as he made his way up to the porch and climbed the steps, stopping in front of her and removing his hat. "Howdy, ma'am," he said. "My name is Woodson Cramer. I'm boss-man of this crew. I'm here to run this ranch, if we can come to terms."

She studied the man. She stood a good half-foot taller than the cowhand, but she could see he was not intimidated in the least by her stature. "I thought pay was agreed upon when Jack spoke with you in Santa Fe."

"For the hands. Foreman gets twice. Are you agreeable?"

Arrogant little bastard. But he was ruggedly handsome with thick, sandy hair speckled with gray flecks. Needed a shave but should clean up nicely. "I suppose so. That doesn't seem unfair."

"And my crew takes orders from me—nobody else."

"I am your employer, Mr. Cramer. I expect to give the orders."

"You can call me Woody, ma'am. And I understand. I'm ex-Army. Top sergeant with Mackenzie. I go by chain of command. You tell me what you want done. I tell my men."

"I have no problem with that. But Jack Moreau here is my second-in-command. You will accept his orders as well."

Jack stepped forward and extended his hand. "I'm Jack. We talked in Santa Fe."

Cramer took his hand in a firm grip. "I remember. You're not one that a man forgets. I accept you stand a step above me, and I am okay with that. Now, can we find some grub here? We rode most of the night. Some breakfast and a few hours nap for the boys, and we'll be ready to go to work. Maybe we can talk after breakfast about what you want done first."

Jack directed Beast to show the new arrivals to the bunkhouse. After Cramer rejoined his crew, Jack returned to where Lilith stood. "I had best move my stuff out of the bedroom tonight."

Lilith said, "Yes. Just in case. I think it would be good for me to own him. And it might take more than money to buy his loyalty."

"He's dangerous. I don't think he would take kindly to being played for a fool."

"I won't deceive him. I'll figure out how to give him a stake in this game, so he won't turn on us if things get tough. Now, let's see how my husband is faring today. With the crew's arrival, we can commence dealing with his stubbornness."

They went back into the house. Lilith was pleased to see Raphael in the kitchen fumbling with some pots and pans. She noted her eldest child was shirtless and barefoot and that his beltless britches did not quite cover the crack of his ass. He was a remarkable physical specimen, she thought. He was ruthless enough to be a worthy successor to her fortune, but she worried he would not outgrow his tendency toward indolence. And she had little hope that age would improve his mind. He was not dimwitted, but she feared someone would always have to tell him what to do.

Thinking of Raphael triggered thoughts of her other children. Margo was an enigma to her. She had always been a sensitive girl, quiet and soft-hearted, with a special affection for animals. Margo worshipped her father who had never tolerated the girl's whippings by Lilith when he was available to intervene. The girl was bright enough, but Lilith found her easy to intimidate and took some pleasure in keeping her daughter constantly on edge and fearful of her mother's unpredictable flashes of temper.

Gabriel had caught Lilith off guard, though. She believed her younger son had the family's keenest mind—next to her own, of course. But she had thought him under her iron hand and had been caught off guard by his escape with Margo and the slut Adam claimed was his wife. Gabriel had turned out to be a sneaky bastard like his father, but she was still willing to find a place for him in her spiderweb of business enterprises, a position where he would be no threat to her authority. Adam had doubtless engineered the flight from the ranch. Beast and Hugo admitted Gabriel had spoken to his father the night of their arrival, claiming she had authorized the visit. When she learned of this, she had exploded and shredded the fools with her razor-sharp tongue, finally giving them a shot at redemption by sending them on the aborted recovery mission.

When they reached Adam's present room, which had formerly been occupied by Margo, Lilith said, "Check his chains, and then leave me alone with him. We need some husband and wife time."

When they entered the room, they found Adam Laurent lying on his back with his right wrist chained to one of the ornate iron rods decorating the headboard. His eyes were fixed on the ceiling, and he seemed not to notice them. He was shirtless and wearing only a pair of baggy undershorts. Moreau stepped over to the bedside and examined Adam's wrist. "Manacle's a bit tight maybe, but it won't kill him."

"Then we'll leave it for now. And the anchor?"

Moreau tugged on the chain that was fastened to the rod. "He's not going anyplace."

"Tie his other wrist to the headboard, too. Check the closet. Margo should have a belt or scarf that you can bind him with."

"The chain will hold."

"I must have the other hand bound for what I have in mind."

"Lilith, for God's sake. Not now. Think about this."

Jack Moreau was the only man on earth who could question her without fear of retribution. "Do I have to do this myself?"

He looked at her with exasperation. "I'll see what I can find."

In a few moments he turned away from the closet with a narrow braided-leather belt. He walked silently to the bedside, grabbed Adam's wrist and knotted the end around it. Adam resisted only briefly, easily overpowered by Moreau's muscular arm. When Adam was bound tightly, Moreau stepped back.

"Light me one of your cheroots, and then you may leave, Jack," Lilith said.

Moreau reached into the breast pocket of his shirt, plucked out a small cigar, then stuck his hand into his trouser pocket and removed a match. He struck the match on the metal headboard, placed the cigar between his lips and lighted it, taking several puffs before he passed the cheroot to Lilith who pressed it to her lips and drew deeply, savoring the taste before allowing the smoke to slowly seep from her mouth while Moreau made his exit.

"I am going to have breakfast," he said as he stepped through the doorway and closed the door behind him.

Lilith eased nearer the bedside and looked down at Adam who lay there watching her warily.

"You haven't been very talkative," she said.

"We don't have anything to talk about," Adam replied. "You will round up your thugs and ride out of here, if you have any good sense left in you."

She had hoped that after a few days' incarceration, Adam might be more docile and reasonable. He did not appear to yet appreciate the gravity of his situation. She sucked again on the cheroot, and while exhaling pressed the sparking tip to his left nipple and held it there, savoring the smell of burning flesh that rose up. Adam gasped and then moaned. Tears came to his eyes, but he did not scream. She raised the cheroot and looked with satisfaction at the raw red and black-crusted brand she had left there.

"You are insane, Lilith," Adam said, his voice a near whisper. "Why are you doing this? What does it accomplish?"

After another puff, she repeated the assault on his other nipple. This time he groaned, writhing in pain. He kicked and tried to roll away, but she held fast until Adam broke out in a cold sweat, and she had done her damage. "I am branding you, Adam. I own you, and you failed to understand that. You are an adulterer. The law says you are my husband, and the whore you have been humping is just that—as her Mexican friends would say, a *puta*. The child she carries is devil's spawn until I kill it. You have my brand now to remind you forever that you are my property. And I am not finished."

She grasped the waist of his undershorts and tugged upward, peering underneath and smiling. "Little fellow is hiding, isn't he? I suppose I will have to brand him, too, if you do not become more cooperative." She knew that the true male Achilles heel was found in a man's drawers, where most of them kept their brains as well.

She could see she had claimed his undivided attention now. Adam spoke in a raspy voice. "I don't know what you want. You showed up here and took over the ranch. But it's not yours, and I won't be going back to New Orleans with you. Never."

"I could take you back in a coffin, but that would be a wasted effort. But you have a debt to pay. You stole from my bank accounts, and you took my daughter."

"I did not touch your accounts. My name was the only one on the accounts I closed, and the funds were from my personal investments."

"But you hid them from me."

"You had your own accounts and investments, and my name was on nothing. Your assets dwarfed mine. You tried to keep me dependent on you. I was like your pet dog, standing by all those years to do your bidding. I owe you nothing."

"You owe me everything," Lilith shrieked, "and I am taking it. I had my New Orleans lawyer inquire into the public records after I received the Pinkerton report on your whereabouts and property acquisition. Your so-called marriage to the Mexican slut does not exist under the law. You did not divorce me. I am your first and only wife. If we divorce now, I am entitled to half of your property in the New Mexico Territory according to territorial law. You have no claim to mine under Louisiana law since you are no longer a resident there. And, if you die, I inherit it all."

"I made a will leaving everything to Angelina."

Fool. That is precisely what she wanted to know. "Under territorial law, the spouse cannot be denied her half, so I guess this woman and I would be partners. I can deal with that. I suspect you did not inform your lawyer that you had a bona fide wife somewhere. More likely, you did not have a lawyer prepare the will. I wonder if the will might even be in this house. If so, it might get lost." It was nice to see some real fear in his eyes. The will was obviously nearby, likely in his office. She lifted his undershorts again and dropped the smoldering cheroot stub inside. Lilith then did an about-face and walked out of the room leaving the sound of Adam's screams behind her.

Chapter 18

I T WAS FOUR o'clock, official closing time for the Second National Bank of Santa Fe, but the door would remain unlocked, and the armed guard inside the door would remain on duty for another hour until bank president Willi Spiegelberg and junior vice-president Rylee O'Brian departed. The Spiegelberg family tried to accommodate customers whenever possible, and Willi and Rylee did not hesitate to assume teller duties after hours if it would help a local businessman or rancher.

Willi occupied the only private office in the bank, which had been established initially in a corner of the Spiegelberg Mercantile store. Now the financial institution enjoyed the privacy of its separate space in an adjacent building. Rylee and the senior vice-president worked in three-walled partitioned areas opening on the public areas so they could observe activity at the half dozen teller windows and be easily accessed by customers.

Customarily, at the end of each workday Willi dropped by Rylee's desk to chat about the day's business. She knew he just enjoyed her company. He was not a lecher. She felt she was the daughter he never had. Today, he sat down in front of her desk, looking a bit tired after a long day, but his suit and tie were unwrinkled, looking as fresh as at the day's beginning. She wondered how he avoided the crumpled look that the other bank employees took on as the day passed.

Willi slumped in the chair and ran his fingers through his thick, graying hair. Rylee figured he was in his early fifties, an old man from her perspective. His chin sagged a bit, and he carried a modest paunch, but he was reasonably fit for a man who had spent a lifetime in a sedentary occupation. "I had a letter today from my friend Big Mike Goldwater in Phoenix."

She did not have a clue where this was leading. Michael Goldwasser, Anglicized Goldwater, was a Jewish trader friend of the Spiegelberg brothers. Willi occasionally chided the legendary trader for lacking in refinement, since Big Mike was of Polish Jewish heritage, unlike the Spiegelbergs, who were German Jews. Big Mike and his brother, Joseph, had recently established a large mercantile in Phoenix under the name of J. Goldwater & Bro. "And your friend has some important news?" she asked.

"Within a few years Big Mike hopes to buy out his brother's interest in the business. Mike's sons, Morris and Baron, would then take over day-to-day management of the mercantile. But Big Mike has another venture he would like to pursue . . . banking. Of course, he cannot abide being outdone by the Germans in Santa Fe. This, however, has not kept him from seeking our counsel in establishing such an enterprise. He has asked us to send one of our officers to Phoenix to help in organizing such an institution."

"Charles Bender is a bachelor, knows the business and would be very capable. How long would he be absent from the bank here?"

"It would require about six months, perhaps slightly less. But I don't see this as a task for our senior vice-president. I think Riley O'Brian is the perfect person for this job."

"Me? I cannot imagine."

"Hear me out. He will pay twice your salary here."

Willi had snatched her attention. "But do I know enough? And would he listen to a woman? Especially one my age?"

"He might be wary at first, but Big Mike will listen to anyone who can make him a dollar. But it might take you an hour to capture his full attention. This would be a tremendous experience for you. My only concern is that he will try to steal you away."

"Oh, no. I love Santa Fe, and, though I cannot say I would never leave, I am far from ready to leave my adopted family. Besides, I have much to learn from you yet, and you and your brothers have provided me with more opportunity than I could have dreamed of when I came here as a fifteen-year-old."

"And we will try to furnish enough opportunity in the future that you will not be tempted to leave us."

"When would I go to Arizona?"

"Likely October. You would spend the winter there, which I am told is more than tolerable. There are details to be worked out. For instance, we are going to propose that he sell us ten percent of the shares, and your assistance will be conditioned on his acceptance. He will complain about the German Jews who rob him, but he will accept. Please understand, you are not required to accept this assignment. You may have a few weeks to decide."

"That sounds fair enough." But she was already making plans for her visit to Phoenix. "Mr. Spiegelberg, I would like to ask you about something completely unrelated to banking."

"Rylee, when are you going to call me 'Willi'? Mister makes me feel ancient."

"I will start on my twenty-first birthday. I promise."

"That's almost three years, but I will not debate the matter. What is your question?"

"Have you ever heard of Adam's first wife?"

His brow furrowed. "Are you speaking of the Old Testament Adam . . . from the book of Genesis? We call the primary holy book the Tanakh."

"Yes. I have a friend who would like to know the story."

"Well, you will not find it in the holy books of any religion that I know of. But it is a legend attributed mostly to those of Hebrew persuasion that shows its face from time to time. Why did you not ask Jael? By the way, she owes me a visit to converse an hour or two in Yiddish. It is good for us both to practice this ancient tongue from time to time."

"I shall remind Jael. She will be living in Santa Fe permanently now and should be able to see you more often. But, as for Jael, I did ask her, and she said she had never heard of it. Remember, though, that she was taken by Comanche at age thirteen. While her parents were Jewish—good German Jews, I think—she thinks of herself as Comanche, not Jewish, and is still much taken by the Comanche religions."

"Ah, the age-old question. Does being Jewish refer to a race or a religion? But you asked about the legend. Yes, I have heard it on several occasions, and I can tell you there are a few who swear to the truth of it. I cannot argue the point. Faith is a belief one cannot prove. But, for my own comfort, I will refer to Adam's first wife as a creature of Jewish mythology. Her name was Lilith, and she did not appear in any writings until around the fourth century. In the folklore of that time and several centuries later, it was said that she was created at the same time and from the same clay as Adam. This contrasts with Eve, who was created from one of Adam's ribs. It was written that she left Adam after she refused to be subservient to him and then would not return to the Garden of Eden after she had coupled with the archangel Samuel."

Rylee asked, "In the mythology, did Lilith have children with Adam?"

Willi chuckled, "It depends on the version of the story. Some say there were none. Others say there were several who joined her when she left Adam. She was a very wanton woman." He hesitated, and his face turned tomato-red. "It was said that her appetite for males was insatiable. She and Adam fought because she insisted that since God made them from the same clay, they were equal and—" and Willi's face turned scarlet again. "She should lie on top when they . . . I cannot say it. Anyway, when he refused, she left him. One text said she killed her own children, although I am not clear on why she did this. Different cultures had varying versions of Lilith. In several language texts, the term "lilith" is translated into "night creature" or "night monster," and some feared Lilith would come during the night and take and kill their children."

"So there are many versions of Lilith's story?"

"Oh, yes, but they have persevered throughout history. There are paintings of artist's perceptions of this incredibly beautiful, seductive woman. A few sculptures, I believe. A good German, Goethe, in his work *Faust*, wrote of the dangerous Lilith. Her myth has endured."

"Are there some who believe she had descendants?"

"Absolutely. There are certainly many witch covens that worship Lilith and witches who claim to be her grandchildren. Some believe she became a vampire. One of the most persistent stories is that her descendants have the capacity to transform themselves from wolf form to human and back again. Supposedly, there are colonies of such creatures scattered about the world."

"They are called wulvers. It is said there is a colony in Scotland."

"Yes, I have heard that story. How did you learn about it?"

"My friend mentioned it."

"I would like to meet this friend of yours."

"I hope you can someday. Thank you for your enlightenment. I knew if anyone knew the story of Lilith, you would."

He laughed. "I'm glad she is just a story. I would not want to encounter this woman or any of her descendants."

Chapter 19

WOLF AND HIS makeshift posse set up camp an hour after sundown. This was their second night on the trail. He had camped at this place about ten miles northwest of Taos several weeks earlier at the beginning of his artistic excursion. He had been comfortable riding later than usual since the cool evening did not tax the mounts so much. He was familiar with this secluded spot nestled in the mountains with spring water escaping from a crease in a granite wall and flowing into the nearby stream. There was ample grass for grazing the horses and no reason not to build a fire. Considering the rugged mountainous terrain, they were seven or eight hours from the Bar P valley, he calculated, and it was time to talk.

Josh and Mose prepared a supper of bacon, beans, and biscuits while Wolf and Gabriel tended to the horses and collected water to replenish supplies. The conversation was sparse and casual until after they ate. Then, the men, holding tin cups of hot coffee, gathered around the fading embers of the fire which still cast a soft glow on their faces. Wolf spoke softly, "I would like to saddle up by sunrise so we can reach the Perez grant by mid-afternoon at the latest. Gabe, what happens if we ride in and just demand to talk to your father?"

Gabriel said, "I think we will all be shot down like dogs."

"Even if we make it clear we are representing the law?"

"That would make no difference to Mother. She would just make certain she killed us all. The bodies would be disposed of so they would never be found. She would deny she ever saw us."

"She wouldn't kill her own son?"

"Now that I have betrayed her, she has likely decided I am no longer her son. Do not delude yourself that she has normal human emotions. I don't understand it all, but she thinks of herself as more than human. It is like she views herself as a divine creature of some kind. She is my mother, and I hate to say it, but I believe she is totally without conscience. She is very intelligent, but she is sometimes blind to the reactions and feelings of others when she is focused on her mission of the moment.

She is invincible, you see. She was caught by total surprise when my father departed with my sister. It just did not occur to her that Father would dare challenge her authority. But when it happened, she became obsessed with finding him and exacting retribution."

Wolf said, "You told me she has three hired guns."

"Yes. Pedro, Beast, and Hugo. Then there is my brother, Raphael. He is more than competent with a rifle and pistol. He will obey Mother without question. The most dangerous of all is Jack Moreau. He is a master of all weapons, and a man of unmatched agility and strength. He has been Mother's right hand since childhood and would die for her in an instant. And, of course, Mother can handle a gun better than most men."

"And you said a ranch crew should be there by now?"

"Six men or more. The question is how many men would stand with her against the law. Maybe none. Maybe all."

Wolf asked, "Is there any chance your mother would surrender peaceably?"

"No."

"And you are certain she killed your father's ranch crew?"

"I have no doubt in my mind, but I did not see the bodies. I did see the body of the woman Pedro killed, though."

Josh interjected, "Before I went home, I went to Judge Ritter's office and swore out a federal search warrant, not that most peace officers worry about that nicety. This would put us in a solid legal position to search the property."

Wolf said, "Sometimes a law wrangler can come in handy. The tricky part is serving that warrant and convincing this woman to comply."

Josh said, "If we ride in as a group, it's a huge risk. They will see us coming and have time to set up an ambush. And they will know just how many guns we've got."

Gabriel said, "I think I should ride in alone. I can find out what's going on and let you know some way."

Wolf said, "You told me your mother was capable of killing you. I'm not sure this is a good idea."

"She is capable of doing it, but if I show up alone, she will be curious. She will want to know what happened to Angelina and Margo. She will devise a way to punish me for my disloyalty, but she won't do that till she gets her questions answered, and I won't be quick to respond. If I stay through the afternoon and night, I should be able to size up the numbers she can count on to back her, figure out where everybody's at and get back to you before sunup the next morning."

Wolf shook his head. "I don't like the odds here. Where do we hide out in the meantime?"

"There's a hogback ridge that runs northeast of the hacienda. We hid behind it before we moved in and overtook the place. There's no way they can see you there, and I can slip out and get back to you. Besides, I can't wait any longer. I've got to know what happened to Father while I've been gone."

Moses Monroe said, "Let me go with him. He can say he hired this old darky to help find his way back here. His mama won't believe he come back by his lonesome. I'll say I'm looking for work—maybe in the stable. I saw the woman before at The Exchange stables. She didn't pay no mind to me. Folks like her don't notice old black men forking horseshit from the stalls."

"She'll take your rifle first thing," Wolf said.

"Get me another when I need it." He pulled up a trouser leg and pointed to the sheathed knife strapped to his skinny calf and caressed the bleached bone handle.

Josh said, "It makes some sense, but I think if they get in there without being shot to pieces, they ought to stay put. We would have two inside to do damage if they need to. Then we ride in with a warrant to search the place.

They might still be spooky about taking down a federal marshal and his deputies, so it will be your call, Marshal, on whether to make arrests or return with more guns. Regardless, we don't ride away without Adam Laurent."

"Your idea makes some sense," Wolf replied. "Let's grab some shuteye. We can talk about the details of this dubious strategy on the trail tomorrow. If anybody's a praying man, it might be a good time to send a word to the fellow upstairs."

Chapter 20

MOSES MONROE AND Gabriel Laurent rode their horses toward the Perez hacienda at a slow trot, not wishing to excite any observers or cause any alarm. Looking out over the valley, in the distance Gabriel could make out the movement of at least three cowhands riding along the fringes of one of the herds. "What are the riders doing with the herd?" he asked Mose, who had the appearance of a slouched scarecrow in his saddle. "I know nothing about the cow business."

"Likely just checking for any critters what might be sick or hurt, especially the calves. Maybe taking a rough count. Don't matter none to us except that's three fewer to give us trouble here. I was thinking, though, that it might help some if Oliver and Josh could get a few such riders out of the way before they come in tomorrow. Anyways, it's better to have them out there than up close if trouble comes."

Gabriel nodded toward the big house. "On the veranda. The woman standing there is my mother."

"Looks like a big red bird. She got feathers?"

"Don't ask her that. The tall man next to her—that's Jack, the one I mentioned."

"Fearsome looking feller. You didn't mention he was a black man."

"Never thought about him that way. Most of us in New Orleans are some of about everything. Like my family, Jack—his real name is Jacques—has got some French strains. My father's pretty strong on the French side. My mother has got a few black ancestors with some French and a fair dose of Spanish. I tried to figure out once what part of everything I was and gave up."

"Hell, boy. Some won't admit to it, but most of us are mixed up somehow. Look at my old dark hide. You would never guess I got me an Irish grandpa. Of course, he never would have claimed me. But he's why I ain't as black as some colored folks."

Lilith's voice broke into their banter, as she yelled from the veranda. "What the hell are you doing here, Gabriel?"

Gabriel waved as they approached. "Good morning, Mother."

"You cowardly clump of cow shit. You ran out on me. Turned traitor. If you were coming back, you should have brought your sister and the whore with you. And who's the nigger?"

"This gentleman's name is Moses Monroe. He offered to help me find my way back here. He's looking for work. He knows horses. I thought he might be handy in the stable."

She looked at Mose and seemed to be appraising him like a horse on the auction block. "You sure as hell are a sorry-looking thing. Can you cook? I don't need a stable-boy. I'm looking for somebody who can cook without cremation."

Mose replied, the tone of his voice deferential, if not subservient. "Yes, ma'am. I done chuck wagon duty for two cattle drives north from Texas. Nobody died from my cooking. Nobody complained neither."

She turned to Jack. "Take this darky to the kitchen. Tell Pedro that Monroe is head cook until I say otherwise. Pedro will be his assistant. Raphael can get rid of his apron and buckle on his gunbelt again."

After Mose dismounted and followed Moreau through the door, Lilith nodded to a short man Gabriel did not recognize. He had been watching them suspiciously from his position under a pine tree off the far end of the porch. "Woody, have one of your boys put up the horses. Get their rifles from the scabbards and put them in the office. Any ammunition in the saddlebags, too. Gabriel, take off your gunbelt and hand it to Woody. Then come in the house with me. We'll talk while I decide what to do with you."

So far, Gabriel thought, his mother had been remarkably restrained. That only meant she was holding back her fury until she elicited the information she was after. But if he danced around her inquisition carefully, it seemed she might settle for punishment ending short of death. Hopefully he could defer the sentence until after Oliver and Josh arrived. Gabriel dismounted and climbed the veranda steps to join his mother.

The man called Woody brushed past him, carrying his and Mose's weapons. He noted now that the man was one that women would likely find handsome, his waist slender and compact but shoulders and chest heavily muscled. He wondered if his mother found the man attractive. He had no illusions that she had ever been faithful to his father. But she had been insanely jealous of any female who indicated an interest in Adam Laurent. He recalled a buxom servant girl who had obviously been enamored of his father. She had been quick to anticipate his father's need for a drink or snack or any other comfort and, even under Lilith's watchful glare, had behaved flirtatiously. He was certain his father had not participated in any dalliance before the young woman was discovered mysteriously dead in her bed one morning. Authorities found no marks on her body to indicate violence or foul play of any sort. His father had been terribly sad about the tragedy, but Lilith had walked the mansion halls as if the incident was no more than a glass of spilled milk, showing traces of an icy smile on her face.

He had taken no more than a few steps trailing his mother into the living room when the blow struck him behind his neck and sent him reeling to his knees. He turned and saw Raphael's twisted lips and enraged stare before the fire iron clutched in his brother's hand swung again and caught his forehead with a glancing blow and flattened him on the hardwood floor. His head was spinning now, but he caught a glimpse of his mother seating herself in a chair to watch whatever was playing out here. And it infuriated him.

He looked up though blurry eyes to see his brother hovering over him like a bear ready to finish its kill. "You like that you cowardly son-of-a-bitch? A dose of what you gave me. Well, I've got more of it. We're just getting started." It struck Gabriel then that this was beyond a brotherly squabble. Raphael was set to kill him. No quarter. And his mother was going to sit by and watch. The thought cleared his head some, just before the point of the heavy iron rod drove toward his chest. He rolled and felt a searing pain as the point tore the flesh covering his ribs. Before Raphael could pull his weapon back for another strike, Gabriel's fingers closed over the iron's shaft and clutched it with a near death grip. Raphael tried to yank it away, but Gabriel held fast and was lifted off his back.

He stumbled to his feet, still hanging onto the fire iron, as he struggled to wrench the weapon from his brother's hand. Finally, he suddenly let loose, and Raphael's momentum launched him backward, his buttocks thudding on the floor and the fire iron slipping from his grip and tumbling out of reach. Gabriel leaped on Raphael like a mountain cat, ignoring the blood soaking his shirt and streaming down his side. He pinned his confused brother's shoulders to the floor and then drove a fist into his nose, hammering Raphael's face again and again. Twice, Raphael lifted his head, and Gabriel slammed it back against the floor. Suddenly, he was aware of his brother's shrieking and his own bloody fists. He stopped instantly, shocked by his own rage. "I am not my mother," he whispered. "Dear God, do not let me be my mother."

Gabriel pushed himself away from Raphael, and clambered to his feet, taking several steps before collapsing in the nearest stuffed, leather armchair. He sat there, catching his breath and trying to gather his wits, only vaguely aware of his brother's moaning a few paces from his feet. He looked around the room until his eyes met Lilith's.

She had an incredulous look on her face. "I wonder if I have misjudged you," she said.

Then he saw Woody standing silently in the doorway, studying him with interest. Lilith saw him also and said. "Tell the darky to get his ass out here and tend to Gabriel. Then help me get Raphael into the spare bedroom."

Chapter 21

LILITH SAT IN what she now considered her office in the house, experiencing a rare introspective moment. Ordinarily she never second-guessed herself, refusing to acknowledge errors or poor decisions. She just forged ahead and shifted strategies to get whatever result she sought. She allowed nothing to stand in the way of her plans. But she found herself wondering now if the New Mexico journey had been ill-advised.

For several days she had pressured Adam to handwrite and sign a will that left the land grant property to her. She could write up such a will and have him sign it, but her lawyer had told her several witnesses would be required if the entire document was not written in his own hand, and she was not willing to rely on the testimony of such persons in a court of law. Regardless, he was refusing to sign any such document, insisting it would be his own death warrant. She had given up on the burnings. His male parts had become a mass of red scars, which gave her some satisfaction, and he had not given in when she extracted his toenails.

She had a fair chance of inheriting in the absence of a will, but her three children would take a half share. Raphael would not be a problem, but her discovery that Gabriel was not the namby-pamby she had thought troubled her. He would not lightly surrender his interest in an estate nor would he allow Margo to do so. Her greater concern was that Adam had another will secreted away that could only be revoked by a subsequent will. In that case she could claim a spousal share by proving she was Adam's rightful widow, but she would end up owning half the ranch with the will's beneficiary, presumably Angelina Perez. She shrugged. She supposed she could force a sale of the property and return to New Orleans with a nice bundle of cash. She was not about to spend the rest of her life in this godforsaken country anyway. It was not just the land. The people were strange and unpredictable. She found their motives and intentions difficult to evaluate, their loyalties less certain. She would settle for what she could and get the hell on her way. But Adam had to die first. And very soon.

She looked up at the sound of someone clearing his throat. Gabriel stood in the doorway, hat in his hand and his head wrapped with a bandana that did not quite cover all the swollen flesh around the wound Raphael had inflicted with the fire iron. His shirt, one side covered with brown drying blood, drooped over his slender, sinewy frame. This was not a boy, she realized, but a full-grown man, and he would be easy on the eyes for any young woman. How had she not noticed this before?

"Sit down," she said, nodding at the straight-back chair in front of the desk.

Gabriel sat down but said nothing.

"The wound in your side. Is it serious?"

"No. Mr. Monroe sewed it up and greased it with something. A dozen stitches, maybe. How is Raphael?"

"You made a mess of his face. Broke his nose. The entire back of his head where he struck the floor is swollen, and he just babbles. He is in bed, but I told him to get out of it in the morning. Stay away from him. He will try to kill you someday."

"I am sorry about that."

"Why? He tried to kill you."

"And I might have killed him if I had not come to my senses."

"You may come to regret that you did not."

"You did not even try to stop us."

"No." Why should she have? It was very exciting. "Now, we must talk. Where is your sister and the whore?"

"Santa Fe."

"But where in Santa Fe?"

"I can't say."

"Can't or won't?"

"Take your pick."

"Getting a smart mouth, it appears." She could feel her rage simmering, but she knew she must subdue it. "Is your sister coming back, too?"

"I think not. Certainly not while you are here. That goes for Angelina, too, of course."

"I suppose they went to the law?"

"Yes, I took them there. Tried to speak to the United States Marshal."

"Tried?"

"He was gone on business. He was to return yesterday, as a matter of fact. Angelina hired a lawyer who will get the marshal out here. He should be here with a posse of twenty men as early as tomorrow."

Lilith did not know whether to believe him. There was a time when he would not have dared lie to her, and she would have read the lie in his eyes if he did. But she did not know this young man, and he was playing this game with a perfect poker face. "The marshal will find nothing here. He cannot remove me. I am your father's wife."

"I told the lawyer that innocent men were murdered here. The marshal will investigate. If there were no killings, I suppose you will be permitted to stay for now."

"You are not here to help me, are you?"

"No."

"Then why did you return after betraying me?"

"I don't consider it betrayal. I prefer to think I saved you from committing another murder."

"Then why did you come back?"

"To see Father. In fact, I would like to see him now to assure myself you have not harmed him."

"He is doing well. I have cared for him appropriately. You may visit with him at supper to verify this. I had a steer slaughtered, and I am already smelling cookfires and roasting meat from outside. Perhaps your Negro does know how to cook. The entire crew is eating on the lawn tonight. It promises to be a lovely evening. Suppertime is a few hours away. You may have the run of the ranch yard so long as you stay away from the stable and this house. If you wish to be helpful, you could assist the hands with moving tables from the chuck-house to the yard."

"You sound like we're having a party."

"I have been planning it for several days, but you can think of it as a welcome home celebration." Lilith was thinking of the picnic as Adam's Last Supper.

Chapter 22

J AEL STOPPED AT Oliver Wolf's residence at Danna Sinclair's request to question Angelina Perez Laurent in more detail about the circumstances of her alleged marriage to Adam and the transfer of the land grant to his name. As Jael and Angelina sat on the leather-cushioned settee in the living room, Margo entered with two cups of tea. This pleased Jael, since coffee had been a rarity during her life with the Comanche, and she had never acquired a taste for the bitter stuff. She had concocted many teas during those years, however, some of which had medicinal properties. The girl set the steaming cups on the sturdy cedarwood coffee table in front of the settee.

"Thank you, Margo," Jael said. "I see you found Oliver's teas. He has an assortment of recipes he created for Tabby. He spoils her something terrible."

"Then why did she leave?" Margo blurted out. She lowered her head. "I'm sorry. It is none of my business."

"It's a natural question. Tabby is my best friend. She shared a tipi with Michael and me for nearly a year. We came to know each other very well. The Comanche are sometimes called the nomads of the plains. I want no more of that existence. But Tabby is not ready to settle. I do not know if she ever will be. She is a nomad. It seems she can endure only so much calm before something calls her to another quest. I love her like a sister, but I fear that Oliver will need to let her go so he can claim his own life."

Margo smiled and said, "I would take him in a minute. And I would not insist that he pamper me. I love this house, the furniture, the paintings and sculptures—well everything except that other woman's office."

Angelina and Jael laughed. Angelina said, "It is obvious, I suppose. She can talk about nothing but Oliver. She thinks she is in love with him. And she despised him when he first came to help us."

"I was wrong. I told him I was sorry, and he was very kind about my terrible behavior."

"But he is old enough to be your father, dear. I am glad you have come to like him, but do not think of him beyond your friendship."

"I know someone else who married a man old enough to be her father." Margo plopped down on a chair across the table, arms folded across her chest and lips formed in an exaggerated pout.

Jael decided it was time to turn the conversation away from Oliver. "I stopped tonight to check on you, but I also need to speak with you about legal matters. Danna has been researching your case and has more questions."

"Please, ask anything at all. I will try to help."

"First, you must understand that your marriage may not be legal. Yes, in the eyes of your church, you may be husband and wife since the church apparently does not recognize the first marriage, but there is no record of your marriage being recorded in the recorder's office at the federal courthouse."

"Adam did not want to leave a trail of our marriage for Lilith to find."

"Do you have a certificate of marriage from the church?"

"Oh, yes."

"And where is it?"

"At our casa."

"In a safe place?"

"In a metal box under our bedroom floor. The bed rests on a woven rug that covers the little hatch that matches the flooring. A person would not see it by just lifting the rug and peering under the bed. My father had a safe built into the wall of the ranch office, but Adam felt that would be too obvious for the most important papers."

"What church were you married in? There should also be a record there."

"The Church of the Lady of the Guadalupe. It was a private ceremony with Father Luke."

"Will you give us a letter to Father Luke to prepare another certificate verifying the date of your marriage?"

"Of course."

"Danna believes it should be entered in the public record. She is building what lawyers call a chain of evidence. Marriages in the territory are not required to be recorded to be valid. Most people rely on church records to prove their marriages and births and are unaware of the value in making public filings. The important thing, though, is that we be able to prove a marriage. Understand, however, that Adam's prior marriage might invalidate yours and eventually give Lilith some claim to the land."

"I wonder . . ." Margo muttered.

Jael looked at the girl, who appeared to have abandoned her sulk.

"What?" Jael asked.

"If Mother's and Father's marriage is registered anyplace?"

"Danna sent a wire to a lawyer in New Orleans to seek a search of the records there."

"Mother told me they were married by Mambo Lucia."

Jael asked, "Was this Mambo Lucia a clergywoman, a preacher in some church?"

"No. That's why I wondered about the marriage. Mother took me to see Mambo Lucia about a year before Father and I left New Orleans. It was scary. We took an old flat-bottomed boat deep into the swamp. It was poled by a little old black man, naked except for something covering . . . his man parts. The bugs and mosquitos were fierce. And then we came to this place on the water's edge where there were four or five thatched huts. Mambo Lucia lived in one of these. She looked like a witch. Wild kinky hair and scary eyes. Scrawny little thing. Very old. I remember her shriveled breasts, because they were not covered."

"Why did your mother take you there?"

"To have Mambo Lucia drive the wicked spirits from me. The ones that made me so disobedient and unwilling to learn about my responsibilities as a descendant of the first Adam and Lilith. I never did know what she was talking about when she got to ranting about that."

"And I gather Mambo Lucia did not drive the wicked spirits away?"

"No, but she scared me so much I wet my bloomers. She chanted in a strange language and danced around me, poking me with a sharp stick and tossing powder that smelled like peppers all over me. She pulled my britches down and whacked my bottom with a switch till it blistered and then hung a dead rat from a cord about my neck, which I had to wear until we left the swamp. It was awful. She told mother to return with me every month for a treatment. When I told Father, he and Mother had a terrible row about it, but she did not try to take me into the swamp again. I think that is when Father started making his plans to leave with me."

"Your information could be important. If there is no recorded evidence of the marriage," Jael said, "it is possible that a woman like this would not have provided a certificate or any tangible proof of the marriage. The law is very unsettled about such things, but it would be a basis for attack. It seems, at the least, this woman would be forced to come to Santa Fe to testify, and that might be a challenge for Lilith to accomplish. And, if she did appear, she might not be the most credible of witnesses. The marriage might be proved a sham."

Angelina moaned and leaned forward and clutched her belly. "Something is not right."

"What is it?" Jael asked.

"Cramps. Pain. But it is okay now, I think."

"Tell me if this happens again." Jael turned back to Margo. "Can you imagine your mother not having papers to prove her marriage?"

"Yes. You must understand. She is very, very smart. But her weakness is details. She decides what she wishes to do, and then she charges ahead like an angry bull and expects everybody to get out of her way. And most usually do. She is not accustomed to being challenged. It is very possible it never occurred to her anyone would question the validity of her marriage. If she says something is so, it is so."

"Well, first we must determine if the marriage is registered. If it is, there is no reason to investigate further."

Angelina sighed. "It is there again. The pain."

Jael said, "Margo, let's help Angelina into the bedroom."

"The baby is coming?" Margo asked.

"Not necessarily. We must make her comfortable and wait. But as soon as we get her in bed, I want you to go next door and tell Rylee what has happened and that she should go to town and find Dr. Rand. Bring Michael back with you."

After they positioned Angelina on the bed, Margo raced out of the house. Jael helped Angelina out of her clothes and into a robe.

"I am afraid," Angelina said. "Have you given birth to a child?"

"No. But when I lived with the Comanche I helped with many births." She took Angelina's hand. "I will be with you until the baby is born. It is impossible to know how long this will take, but you must tell me whenever you have a contraction. And they could stop. We must wait."

"I am having another."

Jael decided she should start preparing seriously, and when Margo returned with Michael, she commenced issuing instructions. Wide-eyed Michael stood in the open doorway next to Margo. "Michael, get a fire started in the cookstove. Then pump at least two big kettles of water. Margo, see if you can rustle up a few old sheets and blankets and a pair of scissors or shears. Then help Michael get the water boiling."

The two disappeared instantly. She was proud of Michael. A few months short of eleven now, he was tall for his age with rust-colored hair and green-flecked brown eyes like his father's. She was the only mother he had ever known, not yet a toddler when his birth mother was killed and he was taken captive and presented to She Who Speaks by her warrior husband, Four Eagles, as a gift to his childless third wife. The Great Spirit had seen fit to unite her with the boy's blood father following the death of Four Eagles during the last days of the Comanche wars.

Angelina gasped and sobbed, "God help me," she whispered.

Jael bent over the bed, pulled back the gown and felt the woman's bulging belly. There would be a baby this evening, she decided, sooner than they wished. "Margo," she called. "Bring a kettle of water as soon as it has boiled. And the sheets."

Margo returned with the sheets, a blanket and scissors, and dropped them on the foot of the bed, staring with horror at the writhing Angelina before wheeling away and heading for the kitchen. By the time she came back with the kettle, Jael had cut one of the sheets into rags and converted the single cotton blanket into four small ones. "Take Angelina's hand, please," Jael instructed. She folded the extra sheet into thirds, tucked it beneath the woman's buttocks and began her examination, first lifting the knees and washing her with the water. The evidence was compelling. The baby was not going to wait for Dr. Rand.

An hour later, Jael held a kicking, screaming baby girl in her hands and began cleaning her little body. She was a tiny thing but apparently healthy. She asked Margo to retrieve one of the improvised blankets. They propped

Angelina up on pillows and placed the bundled baby in her arms just as Dr. Micah Rand walked into the room with bag in hand.

The young red-haired physician with the boyish smile strode over to Angelina's bedside. "Well, it looks like I was too late to earn my fee. How are you feeling, Mrs. Laurent?"

She tugged the baby close to her chest. "Tired. Sore. Happy. If only Adam could see her now."

"May I examine you and the baby?"

"Yes, of course."

Dr. Rand spoke softly and reassuringly as he checked both mother and child. "The little girl is in excellent condition," he pronounced. "See if you can get her started nursing in the next hour or so. If you have trouble with the milk, send someone to tell me, but I don't anticipate any issues. I know you won't believe this, but you appear to have had an easy and uneventful birth, and your midwife here did an excellent job." He turned to Jael. "If you will not make a habit of this, I promise not to attempt to practice law."

Jael smiled. "Agreed."

After Dr. Rand's one-horse buggy headed down the trail that led back to Santa Fe, Rylee pulled Jael aside. "I found Dr. Rand in his living quarters above the clinic. I took the stairs to the outside entrance."

"Yes?"

"Through the window, I could see he had a guest."

"Yes?"

"A woman sat on the settee beside him, and they each had a drink in their hands, and Dr. Rand's fingers were caressing her shoulder."

"I don't understand what this is all about."

"Well, I don't think most folks would consider a woman visiting a man unchaperoned in his home quite proper."

"Good grief, Rylee, the man's nearly thirty years old. I would wonder if something was wrong with him if he wasn't entertaining someone or being entertained. And he is forced to be near the clinic in case of emergencies like we had tonight."

"But the woman was Danna." Rylee hesitated. "You don't seem surprised."

"Where have you been? They have been seeing each other for months." Jael decided not to add that the two often spent the night together.

"I didn't know."

It occurred to Jael that her foster daughter's absorption with business and finance had left her incredibly naïve about romance. At eighteen, Rylee was a woman. Many were married with children at her age, but so far as Jael knew, Rylee had not yet known the joy or pain of even infatuation with a male. She hoped the young woman's naivety did not lead her to a broken heart someday. Though Jael was only nine years older, she loved Rylee, like Michael, as if she were a child of her own flesh and blood.

Chapter 23

TABITHA AND CAL had headed back toward Santa Fe before angling westward. The Rio Grande's waters were shallow and friendly, but when they reached the Chama River, they found it running fast and only a few feet from bank-full because of snow melt higher up in the Sangre de Christos. However, Cal knew the country and found a crossing that barely challenged the riders. "A few more days, if the thaw keeps up, we could forget about crossing up this way. We would've had to go back down Santa Fe way and then on to Albuquerque. Lost two-weeks' time and risked Apache trouble."

"I don't want to go anywhere near Santa Fe right now."

"Law after you or something? You on the run?"

"The law isn't after me. Am I on the run? Maybe. But I can't decide if I am running to or from."

"You always talk in riddles, Little Sis, and I ain't up to sorting it out. Now that we're across the worst of the rivers—at least I'm hoping—I'd like to make camp. Not feeling too good."

They had at least four hours of daylight left, but Tabitha was not burdened with a time deadline for their journey to the Navajo homelands. She had noticed her brother was leaning forward like an old man in the saddle and was breathing heavily, so she readily agreed to the early stop.

They came upon an expansive clearing in an aspen grove only a dozen paces from a stream that tumbled over its rocky bed on a journey to the Chama. Lush spring grass for the horses and Sylvester, the pack mule. When they dismounted, Cal immediately started rummaging in his saddle bags. Trouble was coming soon. She decided to stand fast and face it.

"They're not in here." He turned and glared at Tabitha with wild eyes. "You took my bottles."

"I saw you sneaking around last night with a whiskey bottle tucked in your coat pocket, sucking at it when you thought I didn't see. While you were sleeping last night—fat chance you would've heard Apaches creeping up on us, by the way—I found three bottles you had stashed away and broke them against a boulder. I'll be looking for any others tonight and do the same. No way you'd hear me."

His face reddened with rage. "You had no right. It was my whiskey. And I need a drink. Bad. And you took it all. I got no more." The look on his face changed from anger to panic.

"You told me in Taos not to let you drink—to keep you away from the liquor. I took you at your word."

Tears commenced rolling down Cal's cheeks, and he looked so forlorn she found herself almost regretting she had destroyed his stash. But he would have run out of the stuff somewhere along the trail. She might as well ride on alone as nurse a sick drunk during the weeks ahead. Tabitha turned away and began to unsaddle Smokey. When she had stowed the saddle and tack and staked the gray gelding in the grass, she tossed a glance at Cal, who was now sitting on the ground at the feet of his big bay gelding, head resting on his raised knees.

"Cal," she hollered, "get up off your butt and take care of your horse."

"No. I'm headed back to Taos or maybe ride down to Santa Fe. Buy me a drink. Get me a bottle."

"You're talking a two-day's ride either way—probably more in your shape. In truth, you would never make it. That's fool's talk."

"Then I'll kill myself. I don't want to go on."

She was flabbergasted and speechless. This was the older brother who had always covered her backside. Big. Strong. Tough as a boot. Reduced now to a sniveling, whiny baby. He would not really kill himself. Not Cal Rivers. Or would he?

She walked over to the bay and untied Cal's bedroll from the saddle and spread it out on the grass under the shade of an aspen some twenty feet distant. "Cal," Tabitha said. He did not respond, and she looked down and saw he was sleeping with head drooped, chin on chest. She took the opportunity to slip his Peacemaker from its holster before she yelled at him. "Cal, wake up."

He lifted his head. "Huh? What's the matter?"

"Can you get up and walk over to your bedroll? I can't carry you."

He started to get up and plopped back down. "Can't."

"Then crawl but get over there under the tree."

And that is what he did, stopping and nearly collapsing several times before he reached the tree. She pulled his boots off, and Cal rolled onto the blankets and closed his eyes. In seconds he disappeared into oblivion.

Tabitha unsaddled the bay and staked the horse near Smokey and removed Cal's rifle from its scabbard before stacking the saddle and gear with her own. While she unpacked Sylvester, who was, thankfully, not a contrary mule, she pondered her dilemma. She could not call upon significant experience in the techniques of dealing with drunks. She had seen a drunk stretched out in an alley or on a Santa Fe boardwalk now and then but left that for the marshal to deal with. For whatever reason, brother Josh was a near teetotaler. She had never seen her father or other brothers drink to excess, although she supposed it had happened during their lifetimes. She, like many Santa Fe women, enjoyed a taste of wine on social occasions, but she knew of female drunks only via the gossip that a reporter invariably picked up.

It took several hours to set up camp to her liking. Tabitha pitched two canvas Army pup tents that had seen Civil War duty, gathered wood and built a fire and lined up two Dutch ovens and cooking necessities. She laid out her own bedroll in one of the tents and placed Cal's guns under a buffalo robe she carried for chilly nights. After tossing her personal gear in the tent, she went to check on Cal. Tabitha did not like the condition she found him in. He was not awake, but he was tossing his head back and forth and writhing in his blankets. Streams of perspiration poured down his face. Did he have a high fever? She knelt and felt his forehead but drew no conclusion. She had to get him and the bedroll into his tent. Perhaps he could summon up enough strength to walk to it. She clutched his shoulder and shook it. "Cal, wake up."

His eyes opened and he looked at her as if she was a stranger. "They're after me," he said.

"Who is after you?"

"Comanches. Hundreds of them."

"The Comanche are at peace."

"Not these."

"Cal, we must get you to your tent. Roll off the blankets, and I'll get them spread out and then come back to help you."

He did not appear to comprehend, so she pressed both hands into his ribs, leaned in and pushed. At some level he seemed to understand and rolled over several times as she kept pushing until he slid off the blankets' edge. She took the blankets and made up his bed in the tent. When Tabitha returned, she found Cal was sitting. She considered this a significant improvement until he started to vomit, spewing a brown slime down the front of his shirt and britches before giving in to several rounds of dry heaves. She guessed that the apple butter spread on the noon stop's dried biscuits had furnished the color of the retching.

The spasms finally subsided, and Cal sat in a daze. Good Lord. She was dealing with a child. She was going to have to treat the big ox like a toddler, it appeared, even to the extent of getting him undressed and dressed again. She was conflicted. On one hand she was sad for his misery. On the other she was outraged that he had permitted himself to slide into such a condition. Yes, his life had taken some bad turns, and she guessed he had drowned his sorrows in the demon alcohol. But she had little patience for victims of any sort. She knew too many, including Jael, her closest friend, who had refused to be defined by victimhood.

She went to Cal's large buffalo-skin bag, where he kept most of his clothing and dug out the only clean shirt, clean only in the sense it was not vomit-covered, and a pair of greasy denims. She also grabbed a pair of red long-johns, thinking he might sleep in those and that the other items might not be needed this evening. When she walked back toward Cal, she thought he looked a bit more alert. "Stand up," she ordered.

Her brother struggled to his feet. She stepped to him and began to unbutton his shirt. He helped some as they stripped the messy shirt away from his torso. She was relieved to see that his sinewy arms and muscular abdomen had not wasted away as much as his frail outward appearance might suggest. Perhaps his physical reconstruction was not so distant if she could get his fool head set straight.

"Now the britches." She unbuckled his belt, gave the buckskins a tug, and they dropped. She gasped and immediately turned her head away. The idiot wore no underpants. She had never in her life viewed any of her brothers' private parts and she wished she could erase this image from her mind. She looked up at her tall brother, who appeared unfazed. "Where are your undershorts?"

He shrugged and started trembling and fell to the ground again. She rarely cried, having grown up fending off the teasing of four older brothers. But she was on the edge of giving in to it now. *Damn you, Cal,* she thought. I should have hired a guide. At that moment she saw the Indian in the trees outside the clearing. And he was moving her way.

Chapter 24

TABITHA TRIED TO gauge whether she had time to race for her tent, where the guns were stored. She decided against it. The man seemed to be alone, and she thought it best not to exhibit any hostility. Momentarily, the Indian entered the clearing leading a strawberry roan stallion trailed by a smaller sorrel packhorse. He was taller than most of the Taos Pueblos she had encountered, dressed in faded denim trousers, ankle-high moccasins and a blue loosely fit cotton shirt over a barrel chest. A red bandana was knotted about his head. She breathed a sigh of relief. She knew him.

"Good afternoon, cousin," the visitor said, looking at the naked Cal and smiling. "I hope I have not arrived at an inconvenient time."

Tabitha flushed, "This is my brother, Calvin. He is having a problem, and your timing could not have been more convenient, North Star. If you will help me now, I will explain later."

North Star tied his horse to a tree branch and joined Tabitha at Cal's side. "He vomited all over his clothes, as you can see," she said, pointing to the garments strewn on the ground. "I am trying to get him into the long underwear and then to his bedroll in the tent."

"He is obviously very ill."

"I guess you could say so. But it's because I took his whiskey and got rid of it."

North Star nodded his head knowingly. "Yes. I have seen this too many times at the pueblos. It is sad. My mother taught my brother, Thunder, and me to fight the demon, as she called it. My father died much too young because of it. Mother calls it the curse of the native peoples, brought by the whites to destroy us. I do not touch the poison."

Cal still sat in the grass, oblivious to the conversation. He was starting to shake now. "He's getting the chills," Tabitha observed. "We must get him covered."

"Yes, but that will not stop the tremors. He will be living in hell for several days. I will reach under his shoulders and hold him up while you work his legs into the underwear."

"Can you lift him? He is so large."

"Not as large as he once was, I would guess. And, yes. I handle many horses. He is just another horse."

She steeled herself for dealing with her brother's nakedness again. She hated that she would be forced to do the intimate work, but she was grateful for North Star's appearance like a guardian angel to save her from desperation.

North Star locked his arms under Cal's shoulders and hoisted him easily from the ground. Tabitha quickly grabbed the long johns and worked her brother's feet into the underwear legs. Finally, Cal seemed to comprehend what was happening and began to help some. Soon he was standing with North Star's help, now attired in his wool long johns. Soon, leaning heavily on North Star, he staggered across the campsite to his tent and collapsed into the bedroll and dropped off to sleep.

"Can you stay the night?" Tabitha asked. "I'll fix some supper while you tend to your horses. Biscuits, beans, and bacon."

"Yes. With your permission, I will stay much longer."

She was uncertain what he meant by that, but she would certainly welcome assistance until she got Cal back in the saddle. "I would be delighted to have you. We can talk after you get settled in. I'm afraid I don't have another tent."

"I did bring my own lodge."

While Tabitha prepared supper, North Star staked out his horses and quickly cut several saplings with his hatchet. Soon he lashed together a shelter frame over which he stretched a cover comprised of various animal skins stitched together. By the time they were ready to eat, he had constructed a dome-shaped lodge that was much roomier than the confining pup tents.

A chill was descending from the surrounding mountain slopes, and Tabitha and North Star inched nearer to the fire's dying embers while they ate. Tabitha faced her cousin from the opposite side of the fire. They both ate ravenously, but she stole glances at him as the coals cast a soft glow on the flawless, bronze skin of his handsome face. She had met him briefly on only two previous occasions when visiting Aunt Dezba. She had found him a quiet, thoughtful and well-spoken person, doubtless thanks to his teacher mother's insistence. His shirt stretched against a muscular frame. She guessed he would be short of six feet tall by an inch or two. He was three or four years older than Tabitha, so she figured he had not quite reached his thirtieth birthday yet.

What was North Star doing here? Unlike his brother, he did not reside at the pueblos. Aunt Dezba lamented she did not see him frequently because he owned and operated a small horse ranch in the foothills some five miles to the north and broke and trained horses for local ranchers. He was evidently something of a recluse who lived a solitary life. His mother said he was a voracious reader and visited her mostly to purchase books that she acquired for him

Her curiosity won out. "I have to ask," she said. "How did you happen to be all the way out here and come across our camp—just when I needed help the most?"

He gave a sheepish smile. "Well, the timing was coincidence, but I did not just happen to be here. I was following you."

"Following us? Why?"

"Mother's insistence, mostly. She sent a message for me while you were staying with her. She knew of my interest in our Navajo ancestors—I have done much reading about their history—and she thought I should accompany you."

"That seems strange."

"As you get to know my mother better, you will learn that she cannot help but meddle into others' lives. I love her dearly, but I need a bit of distance sometimes. She said she wanted me to look after you, but I have read your books about the last days of the Comanche and know you require no looking after. She knows that, too. Her real agenda is for me to find a Navajo wife."

Tabitha laughed. "Why didn't you or she say something before we left? You would have been very welcome to join us."

"I was intrigued by the search for relatives and the opportunity to learn more of our Navajo ancestors and their culture, but I have built a small horse herd—nearly twenty mares now, and I did not know if I could make arrangements for their care. Thunder finally agreed he would move his family to the ranch and look after things until at least late fall. He is also touched by the spirit of the horse, and farming has not worked out well for him. If he does well, I may offer him an opportunity when we return."

"So you will stay with us for the journey? That is a great relief to me. I cannot think of anything that has frightened me more than Cal's sickness."

"And it is a sickness. We cannot allow him to sleep much longer. He must drink and replenish the fluids in his body. Some men in his condition do not survive because they will not take water. I thank you for making the coffee—one of the white man's addictions I have taken on. But I saw you also made a pot of tea. That would be a good thing for him to drink."

"Can you tell me what to expect? How long will this go on?"

"All are different. But we should plan to stay at this place for three or four days at least. The first day is the worst. He will have periods of dropping into a deep slumber but then will later awaken screaming in pain. He will get spells of trembling and shaking. He will sweat away the fluids we are able to get into him. He may hallucinate and become delirious. And he will gag and vomit, although he will have no food to expel. Be prepared for diarrhea. He may be unable to control his bowels and the passing of urine."

"You paint a terrible picture."

"You must be prepared. I have seen this too many times. I sat with one man on three occasions."

"A person would experience this and then choose to go through it again?"

"Oh, yes. Cal must never drink the alcohol again. Ever. Demon alcohol is always teasing and luring her prey to the trap. That will be your biggest challenge: convincing your brother to choose a life outside the bottle. The first step to conquering the beast is to make that choice. Most that I have known do not."

"Get out of here, bitch. Leave me alone, Erin. Give me some peace." The yelling came from Cal's tent.

"It starts," North Star said. "I will try to calm him, if you wish to pour a mug of your tea. It will take both of us to force him to drink. One of us must be within the sound of his voice. Perhaps we can sleep in shifts. He could have a surge of strength and wander off. We can do this together. I promise."

Thank you, Aunt Dezba, for sending North Star, Tabitha thought.

Chapter 25

WOLF AND JOSH sat on the rocky ground behind the hogback ridge, facing opposite directions and resting their backs against an ancient cedar. They had made a cold camp to avoid sighting of a fire by any unwanted observers. The sun had not yet slipped behind the mountains, so with a buckskin jacket it was comfortable enough. But when the sunlight disappeared and the night chill set in, he would be cold. It annoyed him some that Oliver seemed not to notice such things. He had not donned a jacket yet and might not later.

Oliver had been quiet and in something of a mood since they had ridden away from Santa Fe. Josh did not know whether the man was preoccupied with the law enforcement mission or dwelling on his abandonment by Tabby. Or maybe it was nothing at all. But he was betting

Tabby was a big part of it. Surely his sister did not get her craziness from the Rivers side of the family. Probably the Navajo strain. Although he had not noticed that Indians of any tribe were crazier than the white folks who fought them. Craziness was probably universal and could happen to a person of any race or tribe. Then he remembered that Jael had lost her temper and called him crazy when he announced he was joining Wolf on this little mission. They rarely argued, but she had been noticeably put out at him. Likely miffed she had not been invited.

"We haven't heard gunshots," Wolf said from the other side of the cedar. "I take that as a good sign."

"Yeah, quiet is good right now. Did you see cowhands out checking cattle down the valley? If somebody's down that way in the morning, do you think we ought to warn them off before we ride in?"

"If they are far enough out, things should be over, one way or the other, before they could reach the building site after they caught wind of any trouble."

"Meaning gunshots. I don't care for your choice of words, 'one way or the other.'"

"That's how it will be. How good are you with that new Henry rifle you're carrying on the saddle?"

"I've shot it a few times."

"A few times? You brought along a test gun?"

"Well, I gave my Winchester to Michael. I saw this thing at Spiegelberg's and had to own it. It's more of a show gun than anything else."

"A show gun? Why do you call it that?"

"I just purchased some bragging rights. Tabby is always bragging about being the only one in the family to own a Henry. Now I've got one. And I didn't even get a chance to show it to her and devil her about it before she took off." He instantly regretted mentioning his sister's departure, but Oliver took it in stride.

"She would have instantly challenged you to a shooting match."

"That would not have been a good thing."

"Can you handle that Colt on your hip any better than the rifle?"

"Not as well."

"At least you're an honest lawyer."

"I figure any gunplay will be at close range. And I doubt if the duly appointed marshal is a fast-draw gunfighter, either."

"You are right. And that worries me some."

Josh said, "I smell smoke."

"Beef roasting."

"And the law dines on stale biscuits and deer jerky."

"Maybe they'll have leftovers when we ride in later tomorrow morning."

Chapter 26

LILITH AND JACK sat in the ranch office discussing evening plans. "You found a cook," Jack said. "We won't be eating for two hours and the smell of the beef roasting on the spits has got me starving for it. He is working on a banquet it appears."

"I will be checking on progress in the kitchen later. I have a tad of seasoning to add to one of the plates."

"Are you really going to do this?"

"He must die a natural death. Tonight. Gabriel insists on speaking with his father. It would be a huge complication if he does. And I am worried about the law interfering before we complete our New Mexican project. When Adam dies, I will sign a deed for any claim I have in the grant to those men from the Santa Fe League I spoke with. The price will be heavily discounted—I will receive a fourth of the actual market price, but they will take over the legal problems of asserting my claim. With a quit-claim deed, I do not guarantee clear title. They take what I've got, which may be nothing or all. They just want to gain a foothold. I was informed they have lawyers and a small army of enforcers who move in quickly to stomp out any challengers."

Moreau said, "I just don't have a good feeling about what you are trying to do here. Back home, you have enough influence to write your own story. You know who to pay and who to kill. You have a giant spiderweb of protectors in New Orleans. We're piling murder upon murder here, and you don't have any friends outside this room."

"Speaking of friends, has Woody Cramer said anything to you about my proposal?" She was not pleased with the crew foreman. He had not shown the least resistance to her seduction of him when they discussed the outline of a business arrangement a few nights earlier. He had acquitted himself admirably in bed later, but he strangely had not committed to the terms she proposed. When he left after their little tryst, he had simply said he would have to think about it for a few days. She was not accustomed to that type of dawdling after she awarded a man her favors, and the continued delay was testing her patience. If he did not come around by tomorrow, Jack would have to kill the man. She had disclosed too much in her confidence he would leap at the opportunity she offered.

"Cramer has been avoiding me. You offered him five thousand dollars?"

"Yes. If he would organize his crew to help us hold this place against anyone who might try to move us off, law or otherwise, until I got the grant sold."

"That's more than most men like him would make in five years. A lot of men would jump at that kind of money," Moreau said.

"I cannot see why he would not."

"Lilith, there are some honest men and women out there. More than you might think."

She looked at Jack with disbelief. "It is just business."

"Well, I've taken four of his crew aside—men I judged open to doing business. They've signed on with us for a reasonable bonus. Five hundred each up front. Another five when you sell the place and release them. They'll stick to a point."

"What point?"

"Till the odds turn against us. They're the kind who will cut and run and leave the money behind to save their hides."

"What about the other two crew members?"

"I didn't talk to them. They are both Mexicans who see themselves as *vaqueros*, and the others are certain they will not go up against the law. If trouble comes, I'm guessing they'll just hightail it out."

"That takes us back to Cramer. It seems you have stepped in and done his work for him. He's not worth five thousand dollars to us anymore. Kill him at your early convenience but sometime in the next two days."

"I rather like the man, and I doubt he will be an easy kill. But I will keep my eyes open. I would like to do it quietly and hide his body until we can dump it in an arroyo or over a cliff. No shortage of predators in this country to see it disappears quick-like."

"I don't care how, Jack. Just make it soon."

Moreau sighed and nodded.

Chapter 27

LILITH TIED HER long sable tresses back with a red ribbon and examined herself in the bedroom mirror. One of the hands had filled the rusty tin tub hidden in the curtained closet with hot water and would empty and clean it later. She felt invigorated by the bath, but the disgusting tub had triggered a yearning for her civilized life in the mansion outside New Orleans. There she had a porcelain-covered cast iron tub and water closet in her bathroom. Fresh water was pumped through pipes into the house to sinks in the kitchen and several bathrooms. Best of all, she enjoyed the pampering by her servants. She deserved luxury and could not claim it again soon enough.

She walked over to the bedroom window and peered out. The men were starting to gather in the yard. The beef on spits above the cook fires was nicely browned with a few splotches of crusty char. A party atmosphere reigned.

She turned to the dresser, pulled the top drawer out, and reached into the back, searching out the soft cotton bags with her fingers. She plucked one out and quickly checked the tiny sack packed with its lethal contents. The original opening had been stitched tight to avoid leakage. Mambo had assured her that the symptoms from the poison would appear in about one hour and that they would mimic a heart attack. The chosen victim would live no more than a minute or two after onset of chest pain. Half of a bag should be adequate, Mambo Lucia had informed her, but Lilith intended to leave nothing to chance. She hoped to use the entire contents. She stuffed the precious commodity beneath her blouse top between the crevice of her breasts.

She left the bedroom and retrieved her gunbelt and holstered Colt from the peg in the office, buckled the belt tightly about her waist, and then walked purposefully to the kitchen and asked Pedro for a mug of coffee. He complied, but she bristled at the scrutiny she was receiving from the geezer who had declared himself a cook. She wondered if he might not be as dumb as he let on. She took the steaming cup back to the office, where she sliced open the poison bag and emptied the contents into the cup. The powder dissolved nicely, so she took the cup and headed for Adam's room.

When she entered the room, the fear she saw in her husband's eyes pleased her. He probably thought they were going to have another one of their little chats. He lay naked on the bed, his wrists still anchored snugly to the headboard. He was not holding up all that well, she thought. His torso and the bottoms of his feet were a mass of red welts and pock-like marks, his genitals raw and swollen. The mutilations caused by the toenail extractions on one foot were infected and festering with oozing pus. The wounds left by slicing off the tips of his pinkies had scabbed over. While it had all been great fun, the efforts to gain his cooperation had been for naught. Adam had shown strength she had not guessed he possessed. Well, he would be free of his misery soon.

"Adam," she said as she approached the bed, "we're going to let you join us outside for supper tonight. We'll call it a celebration. Gabriel has returned and wants to see you. I told him you could sit together at the supper table and talk as long as you wish. But do not be visiting about our encounters this week. If you do, you risk his life. Think about this. Do you really believe I am not capable of ordering our son's death? You and I are reconciling and will return to New Orleans together. That is what you will tell him. Understand?"

Adam replied with an angry glare.

She pondered calling Jack in to assist, but she did not view Adam in his weakened condition as a threat, and this would be the final intimate interlude between husband and wife. "I brought coffee to perk you up before supper." He would have had nothing to drink since morning so she was confident he would not turn it down. She set the cup on a bedside table. His left side was nearest her and she said. "I will untie your hands so you can sit up on the side of the bed and drink. Your clothes are in the chest. While you are drinking the coffee, I will gather your things and put them on the bed. Then you can get dressed. We cannot have you traipsing out there like this, can we?"

"Why not? Some folks might be entertained. Others not so much so."

"I am untying your wrists now. Don't do anything foolish. Stay put on the bed and drink your coffee." She released one wrist and then the other, ready to step back and draw her Colt if he made a move.

When she finished, she turned to retrieve his garments, and Adam rolled over and sat up, tossing his legs over the edge of the bed. He nodded at his inflamed foot. "I can't get a boot on over your artwork."

She dropped his clothing on the bed. "We will slip socks over your feet, and you can go out that way, unless you have some moccasins in your closet. This isn't a formal ball like we have back home. Now drink your coffee and start getting dressed."

"I don't know if I can pick up the cup. An animal gnawed off my pinkies."

"I regret I didn't cut off your pecker or geld you. Come to think of it, I still might if I don't start getting some cooperation."

"Might as well as much as you've disfigured my private parts."

Lilith laughed, "They weren't that special anyway. I have seen much, much better."

"Yes, I'm sure. A whore has vast opportunities for comparison."

Again, she felt the rage descending upon her. "You are in no position to attack with your hydrophobic mouth." She picked up the coffee cup and handed it to him. "Hold it with both hands. Drink it so you can get dressed and ready for supper."

Adam took the cup in his hands. His usable fingers trembled so much that the warm liquid was splashing over the top. He cocked his head and looked at the cup curiously. "I wish I could have told Angelina one more time how much I love her. Gabriel and Margo, too. Believe it or not, I love Raphael, also, even though he is Jack's."

This was too much. "Drink," she screamed at him.

Adam raised the cup, but before it reached his lips, he tipped it outward and poured the contents on the planked floor between his feet. "Damn. I spilled it." He looked up at her and smiled.

Lilith backed away, expecting him to lunge for her, but he just sat there, apparently too worn down to make a move. But the taunting smile remained, and the Colt was in her hand and the room echoed with the thunder of the first shot before she was conscious of it. The bullet struck him between the eyes, but she was fast on the trigger, and two more shots tore into Adam's chest before he collapsed on the floor.

The door flew open before she holstered her gun. She turned her head toward the sound and saw it was Jack with his Peacemaker in his hand. "Shut the door," she snapped.

Before he obeyed, Moreau stepped out in the hallway, and yelled. "Nobody hurt. Go about your business." He came back in with an exasperated look on his face. "So much for your natural death. What's got into you, Lilith? You haven't been thinking straight since we got here. You let Adam's taking off twist your brain. You can't claim the estate of somebody you murdered. We maybe can buy some time, but the men here are going to figure it out, and there are a few that won't be bought. Besides, what about Gabriel? He's demanding to see his father, and he's been snooping around the place. When Adam doesn't show up for supper, he's going to raise hell."

"We may have to kill him, too."

"Woman, what has got into you? Gabriel's your own son. I don't think more than a few animals, if any, even kill their own young."

"Not even wolves?"

"I don't want to hear about wolves right now. We've got to figure this out. Now. And there won't be any killing Gabriel. I've been doing your bidding most of my life. But it stops there. I've known that boy his whole life. And he's a lot more man than you ever gave him credit for. I won't be a part of his murder. And I won't allow it. You will have to take me down first."

Lilith looked at Jack in disbelief. He meant it. She could not remember when she was last so unnerved. It went against her grain to give in to him, but she conceded she could not unravel the fix they were in without him. "What do you suggest?"

"We make tracks out of here and get to New Orleans the fastest we can. You and me and Raphael."

"I don't know if Raphael can ride after that beating Gabriel gave him."

"We'll give him a day to recover some—if we can. We'll leave after dark tomorrow. Won't tell anybody. We'll just disappear. Take our three mounts and a packhorse. Pack light. I can start packing during the night while everybody's sleeping. We'll be ready to saddle up and make a break sooner if we got to. I'll ask a few questions. Try to find a trail that doesn't push us near Santa Fe. I'm guessing you've still got a fair amount of money in your saddlebags. And I got some. That will help buy our way back home one way or another."

"What do we do with Adam?"

"We can't get him out of here without being seen. After dark the guards we got posted would see us and would conjure up their own explanations if we didn't have a good one. They wouldn't stop us, but word would get out and travel fast. There is what Pedro called a Navajo rug across the hall in the room where we got Raphael . . . where Pedro did his dirty work with the woman. We clean up this bloody mess as best we can, roll Adam up in the rug and push him under the bed. It will take more than a glance through the doorway for anybody to see him then."

She hated to admit it, but Jack was talking good sense. "And Gabriel?"

"We've got to put him out of business till we get out. I came across an old cistern at the bottom of a slope about fifty yards away from the stable, so that puts it twice that from the house and bunkhouse. Not likely he would be heard. Some years back, before they dug a well, the owners built a channel that collected and funneled rainwater for storage in the cistern—probably a backup source for stock. It's a good ten-feet deep with stone and concrete walls, and I couldn't see anything that would make a handhold or foothold for climbing out."

"So we drop him in and leave him there to die?"

"We leave him with a fighting chance. Odds are folks—probably the law—will be searching the place not long after we're out of here. Somebody would hear him or come across him then. I'll drop a few canteens of water in the cistern—maybe a bag of jerky."

"And you just convince him to jump in this pit?"

"Yep. Me and the butt of my Peacemaker. You talk him into coming down to the stable with you when he starts making a fuss tonight, and I'll give him a dose of what he gave Raphael."

Chapter 28

GABRIEL STOOD IN the shade of a towering ponderosa pine, surveying gathering cowhands and gunfighters who lined up at the chuckwagon that had been pulled into the yard adjacent to the ranch house. Looking over the men, he tried to determine which might stand with his mother in a showdown and which might scatter. But he knew he had much to learn about judging men yet. As he had often heard, appearances could be deceiving. His eyes caught one man at the rear of the line, who appeared to be watching his observer. Gabriel did not avert his gaze. He was a short, clean-shaven man with a military bearing, probably about his father's age. His penetrating look was neither friendly nor hostile. Gabriel remembered seeing him at one corner of the veranda when he and Mose arrived.

He figured the sun was probably a half hour away from disappearing over the mountain tops. Where was his father? And Lilith had not made an appearance yet. Their absence made him uneasy. He took comfort in seeing Mose slicing and serving slabs of steaming roast beef from the chuck table at the front end of the wagon. The Mexican stood next to Mose and was ladling out healthy scoops of beans from a kettle. The diners were helping themselves to biscuits from a huge tray at the end of the table and applying generous doses of jam or honey according to their preferences.

He finally saw his mother—easy to spot in her cardinal-red attire—when she broke into the line and offered a plate for the servers to fill. As soon as she had her plate full, she turned and walked directly toward Gabriel. She had a smile on her face, but he knew from a lifetime's experience that could mean anything or nothing.

As she approached, Lilith said, "This plate is for your father. He is waiting in the stable. Went for a walk, and he didn't want to come back and mix with the others. He thought you could talk more privately there. I promised I would leave the two of you alone so you may ask him any question you wish. He will tell you about the agreement we reached. I think you will be very pleased."

Nothing his mother said rang true. "I have been out here since we arrived—why didn't I see you come out of the house?"

"We walked past you, but you were perched at the base of this tree sleeping. Adam asked me not to awaken you. It's up to you. I told him I wouldn't be long, so I must go. Come or not, whatever you wish." She veered toward the stable.

He could not argue the point. He had, indeed, dropped off into a slumber leaning against the tree, sleeping for a good hour or more. Still, why had his father not returned to the house to eat? He decided to nibble at the bait and proceed with caution. Before following his mother, he strolled over to the chuck wagon and spoke to Moses Monroe. "I'm going to talk to my father. Save me a slice of beef and a biscuit or two, would you, Mose?" The lanky, dark man met his eyes and gave a barely perceptible, negative shake of his head. Gabriel knew the head-shake was not a denial of the request but a warning of some sort. Where his mother was concerned, warnings were unnecessary. As he turned away, his eyes met those of the short man, who was next in line for serving. He nodded, and the man returned a nod.

He stayed a few paces behind Lilith as they walked toward the stable. Gabriel said nothing till his mother spoke. "Where is Margo staying? The whore is with her, I suppose?"

Gabriel was tired of this question. He was not about to tell Lilith where the two were staying, but he thought of something that might worry her some. "Margo and Angelina are both being held in protective custody at the United States Marshal's residence."

She stopped and turned her head toward him. "Why on earth would they be in protective custody?"

"We told the authorities that Angelina's life is in danger."

"Why, for God's sake, would you say that?"

"I wonder."

Lilith continued her journey to the stable, walking faster and with deliberation now. When they neared, Gabriel said, "I am not entering the building unless you tell me exactly where Father is at."

"He is just inside sitting on that bench along the wall next to the entrance."

He remembered the bench. He would need to take only a few steps into the building. He caressed the butt of his Colt and followed her inside. He turned and got a glimpse of the empty bench before the jolt against the back of his head dropped him to the stable floor, and he was swallowed by blackness.

* * *

Gabriel awakened to more blackness. The hammering pain in his skull told him he lived. When he lifted his head from the cold stone floor, waves of dizziness and nausea swept over him. He waited in a fetal position until the pain subsided some, and then slowly he lifted himself until he could sit with his back planted against the wall. His fingers tested the wall and floor. Stone with concrete joints, solid and in good condition it seemed. He reached out and felt a corner where one wall met another, which told him he was in a rectangular structure. An abandoned well? He thought of wells as cylindrical in shape, but he could think of no reason why they had to be.

He had no idea how long he had been in this place or what the current hour might be. The Timex watch in his trouser pocket would not be helpful because he would be unable to read the numerals in this darkness. He felt his empty holster and confirmed he had been disarmed. He gently probed the lump on the back of his head— tender, but the blood had dried there, telling him the wound was not fresh. He found himself trembling from the chill locked in by the stone walls.

Not so dizzy now and the pounding in his skull reduced to a tolerable headache, he crawled on hands and knees to investigate his lodging. He prayed silently that he would find no snakes. He feared snakes, all kinds, and Louisiana had more kinds than he could count. At least in New Mexico he had not encountered any tree-climbers.

He came across two full canteens and a small leather bag that contained jerky. He was far from ready to challenge his stomach but was encouraged that his attacker had left survival rations. He took it as an indication there was no imminent plan to kill him. He concluded he was in a structure that was perhaps as much as six feet wide and ten to twelve feet long. He sat and waited and pondered his dilemma until a dusky glow subdued some of the darkness in his prison. He looked up and could see the first light of dawn creeping over the mountains. He guessed it would be an hour before full sunlight kissed the valley.

He leaned back and found himself dozing off when he was startled by a soft voice made hollow and ghostly by walls of his stone chamber. "Hey, kid, are you okay?"

He looked up and saw a hazy face of a man wearing a low-crowned hat looking down at him. "I've been better. But, yeah, I'm okay."

"You got a gun?"

"No. Whoever hit me took it."

"I've got an extra Smith & Wesson, with a box of American cartridges in a bag. I am going to reach down with it. If you will stretch, I think you can grab it and pull it in. If not, catch it when I let loose. Exchange those cartridges for the ones in your gun belt. Give you something to do while you wait."

"Who are you?"

"Woody Cramer, at your service."

"You're the guy that wears the spotted cowhide vest."

"You catch on fast, kid."

"I guess you didn't come to kill me, so why don't you just toss a rope down and pull me out of here?"

"Later, I hope. You're safer here for now. The wrong folks see you, and you're dead meat. And you need to be down there in case anybody comes back to check on you. I'll try to get back with a canteen of water to drop to you."

"Whoever dropped me here—and I'm betting it was Jack—left water."

"Good. Then I won't worry about water. If I don't get back for you, it means you still got serious trouble. Be careful, though, before you use that gun to signal. Be sure it's the good guys out there."

He saw the leather bag with the sidearm and cartridges being lowered. He stood on his toes and reached out with both arms. "A foot short." Gabriel said.

"I'm going to let go."

The bag and contents fell into his open hands and he clutched it and pulled it in.

"Got it. Can I ask you something?"

"I gotta move, kid, so make it quick. Daylight is coming on, and there will be big trouble if somebody finds me here."

"How did you find me?"

"Mose asked me to check on you. We both saw you going to the stable with your mother. When you didn't come back, but we saw her and that big friend of hers leaving the stable, we figured there was trouble. They headed this way for supper with her still carrying that full plate, and that confirmed what we was thinking. I'm a fair tracker, but it didn't take an expert to follow the grooves made by your bootheels when he was dragging you to this place."

"You know Mose?"

"Oh, yeah. From the Exchange stables in Santa Fe. Mose is nobody's fool. He knew I wouldn't sign on to what this outfit is up to. I'm a ranch foreman, not an assassin. He told me about Josh Rivers and White Wolf coming in later this morning. I'll try to get you out before they show up but can't promise."

"White Wolf?"

"That's what he was called when I knew him. No finer scout. No better man."

"My father. Do you know anything about my father?"

"Sorry, son, I don't. All I know is he was locked up in a room in the house. Mose checked the door, but it was locked."

"Okay. Thanks, Mr. Cramer, for helping us."

Cramer apparently had already left and did not hear because there was no response.

Chapter 29

WOLF AND JOSH left their packhorse staked out in the grass behind the ridge and nudged their mounts towards the Bar P building site. They rode the horses at a slow walk, Wolf thinking it best they appear to be casual visitors as they approached. "Two rode out to check cattle this morning," he observed. "I see a few hands lazing around in the yard. Not much of a working ranch today."

As they drew nearer, Josh observed, "Those cowboys lazing around are carrying rifles. I don't think they're hunting rabbits."

"The man on the roof of the hayshed off to our right sure isn't hunting rabbits, and he's got us in his sights." Two men walked out to intercept them before they entered the yard. One, a short, wiry man thick in the chest and shoulders, was trailed by a big hulking figure with a double-barreled shotgun clutched in his bearlike paws. As they approached, Wolf recognized them both. The big man had been one of the Laurent pursuers he had scared off. The other was an old friend, Sergeant Woodson Cramer. He smiled and started to greet Cramer when the serious-faced man cut him off.

"Rein in, gentlemen," Cramer said. "I'm foreman of this outfit. Name's Cramer." His eyes fixed on Wolf's, signaling recognition before he cast a warning glance over his shoulder. "State your names and your business."

Wolf and Josh dismounted before Wolf replied, "I am acting United States Marshal Oliver Wolf." He tapped the marshal's badge that glittered in the morning sun. "This is my deputy, Josh Rivers."

Cramer gave Josh an appraising look. "I know who you are. This ain't your usual line of work."

"Special deputy," Josh said.

Wolf said, "We're here to speak with Adam Laurent."

"Never met the man. But I'm new here."

Wolf thought Woody was telling him that Adam was being held someplace. "Adam Laurent owns this ranch. Who hired you?"

"His wife. Says she's running the ranch now. I guess her husband ain't feeling too good."

"Then I would like to talk to Mrs. Laurent."

Cramer said, "She's in her office in the house last I knew." He turned to the sour-faced man who stood menacingly a few paces behind him. "Beast, why don't you go tell the boss lady that the marshal's here and would like to talk with her."

Beast grunted and trudged back toward the house. When he was out of hearing range, Cramer said, "Ain't seen you since the Red River War, Wolf. I've been in and out of Santa Fe a dozen times and heard about your work there—not the law business—and figured to look you up sometime. Maybe we can talk later, but right now you got a tight spot to squeeze out of."

"And are you in on the squeezing?"

"You know me better than that. I ain't working for this crazy woman. I was going to ride out with two of the boys I brought with me this morning. Then she went and dumped her son in an old cistern."

"Gabriel? Is he all right?"

"Bumps and bruises. And his pride. I talked with him and gave him my spare Smith & Wesson, but I left him there. Thought he'd be safer there till we see how this is going to play out."

"What about Mose?"

"They got him cooking. Folks like Mose have spent a lifetime being invisible. They don't even notice him. They took his guns, but he doesn't seem none too perturbed about it."

"Is this woman going to talk to me?"

"I can't say."

Josh interjected, "We've got a warrant to search this place."

"With or without," Cramer said, "your search won't be done without blood being spilt. She's got seven armed men, besides her and a tall mulatto who is her right hand. She's also got her son, Raphael, but Gabriel beat the shit out of him yesterday, and I don't think he's too fearsome yet."

"Gabriel," Wolf said, "I wouldn't have taken him for much of a brawler."

"I'd guess we all have our limits, and I suppose he reached his."

Wolf said, "I've spotted three guns. Where are the others?"

"Two just inside the house near the door. Of course, Beast is in there now. That's where they've got to be holding the husband."

"Would they kill the husband?" Josh asked.

"If they ain't already."

"What do you mean?"

"There were gunshots in the house yesterday. At least three. Never explained."

Wolf said, "There is no riding away from this. We've got to see what's going on in that house."

"You've got my gun, but I sent the other two boys out to check on cattle. They're brothers and just kids. Just want to be cowboys—*vaqueros* is how they put it. They don't know what the hell is going on here, and I wanted them out of the way if fireworks started. I wasn't about to take them home to their mama wrapped in blankets— saw too much of that through two wars."

"I understand," Wolf said. "I've seen too much blood and death myself, but it seems to keep chasing me. Anyway, here's what I'm thinking. Tell me if you don't like it. I don't think Beast is coming back. Is there a back way out of the house?"

"Yep. One out of the kitchen, one from the office, both on the west side where the outbuildings are located."

"I want to take the house first. Take them down or flush them out. It doesn't matter. Josh, we'll leave Owl and your buckskin here. They won't stray far. Then you and I will walk straight for the door. Woody, you just hang back. They don't know where you stand yet. Rifles won't help us much, but you might make use of one. I'm going to hand you my horse's reins, and, while they're watching us, you just slip my Winchester out of the scabbard and get ready to back us up."

Cramer took the reins and then paused and nodded toward the stable. "Wolf, I swear I just saw the mulatto leading horses out the rear of the stable. It's blocked by pine growth back there. They might be making a break for it."

Wolf sighed. "We're committed to the house. And we take that first." He felt his first objective was to free Adam Laurent and reclaim the property. He guessed it was seventy-five feet or better to the veranda, and he started walking up the slope. "We'd better split," he told Josh. "Make us tougher targets." When they reached the rock pathway to the veranda, he heard two cracks of a rifle from behind them.

"Your friend took care of the guy on the hayshed roof," Josh said from his spot some twenty feet away. One of the gunmen near the end of the veranda stepped out and aimed his rifle at Josh, who crouched, whipped out his Colt and fired. The rifleman's shot went wild, and he grabbed his chest as if trying to plug the fountain that was pumping blood down the front of his shirt. Wolf caught sight of a husky man running for the cover of a buckboard at the edge of the yard. He aimed his Peacemaker and fired. The man stumbled but did not drop until Cramer's rifle fired again and flattened him.

Another gunman tossed his rifle out from behind a Ponderosa and stepped out with hands raised. "Rusty," Cramer hollered, "drop your Colt with the rifle and lay yourself out on the ground and keep your hands where we can see them. Do that, and you might live to see another day."

Wolf heard glass shatter and wheeled to see a rifle barrel poke through the front window of the house. He dove to the ground just before the rifle fired and crawled to the edge of the veranda. The floor was raised at least three feet from ground level, and he figured if he stayed low, the shooters could not get an angle on him through the window. He searched for Josh and saw he had nestled in the same spot on the opposite side of the porch steps. "I thought you couldn't handle that Colt."

"I'm a modest man."

"Any ideas, modest man?"

"I'm just a deputy."

Cramer had moved in closer now, taking cover near the buckboard. He took an occasional shot at the house to keep the gunmen honest. "The men outside were all a part of the crew that came with me. The hard cases are holed up in the house. And, if the witch is in there, she's the most dangerous of the lot."

Wolf pondered the stand-off. Time was wasting. They had to take the house to ascertain Adam Laurent's condition and to begin to unravel this mess. He decided he would crash through the front door with Josh backing him and ask Woody to seek entrance through one of the rear doors. His plan was aborted by the distinctive roar of a shotgun. Silence. Then the front door creaked open, a door Wolf now realized was so thick and heavy he would never have broken through it.

"You all okay out here?"

"Mose?" Wolf asked. "That you?"

"It surely is, Mr. Wolf. Why don't you gentlemen come in? I'll make up a pot of coffee."

Chapter 30

WOLF ASKED CRAMER to retrieve Gabriel from his underground prison while he and Josh commenced a search of the house. Mose held the door open until Wolf and Josh entered the living room, and then closed it. A shotgun was nestled in the crook of his skinny, sinewy arm. "That's Hugo," Mose said, pointing to the body slung backward over a settee, the bloody torso shredded and raining blood onto the polished wood floor, where it pooled and began to spread. "And that's Beast. I think you folks met."

Beast lay stretched out on the floor in front of the window, his head drooping to one side at a peculiar angle because of the depth of the slash in his throat. Wolf noted that from the looks of the floor the man must have been about bled out. "This here is Beast's shotgun." He nodded at the weapon.

"But Beast didn't pull the trigger."

Mose grinned. "Didn't have time."

"Woody said there was one more of the hired guns."

"Pedro's in the kitchen."

Wolf walked into the kitchen and found Pedro on the floor, virtually eviscerated with his belly ripped open from belt to sternum, his open eyes frozen in terror. He went back in the living room where the others had remained. "This woman—Lilith—she's not here, is she?"

"Nope. Her and her man and the boy got the hell out as soon as Beast told her somebody was riding in from behind the ridge. She told them if it was the law, they'd better kill the bastards because they was in neck deep and would be hanging for sure. Guess that was true enough, since they done most of the dirty work, it seems. Of course, them poor cusses in the yard was new to the game. Got themselves killed for nothing."

"Adam Laurent. Is he here?"

"I'm guessing he's here, but I'll be damned surprised if he's alive. I'll show you the bedroom, but it's locked. I know that's where they kept him, but Lilith was in there alone with him late yesterday afternoon, and there was gunshots that shook the whole house. And her man went in there and came back out and told us to stay the hell away and to tell anybody else that came in the same. And

I tell you this: if that devil-witch says to stay away, any man with good sense is going to pay attention."

Mose led them to the door. Another heavy one, and it was, indeed, locked. "Be right back," Mose said. Momentarily, he returned with a big meat cleaver. "Step back, gentlemen." He commenced hacking around the door handle and lock areas and soon wedged the blade through the door and splintered an opening that revealed the latch. He drove a scrawny shoulder that revealed surprising strength into the door, and it gave way and swung open.

Wolf stepped inside and looked around. "Nobody here. Bed is made up."

"Nobody alive here," Mose amended. "It's got the dead smell."

"You're right. It just struck me." Wolf walked around the room, and Josh knelt, lifted the edge of the bedspread and looked under the bed. "Here's the source," Josh said.

Wolf lifted the foot of the bed off the floor to allow Mose and Josh room to maneuver the rug-wrapped corpse out from under its hiding place. The pale mutilated toes stuck out from the rolled rug, giving a strong hint of what was enclosed within. The package removed, Josh and Mose watched soberly while Wolf pulled the rug away from its contents.

Mose said, "Lord have mercy. One shot would have brought the angels. Why three?"

"It doesn't matter. It's what they did before. The toes. The fingers. The burn scars all over his body. He was blinded in one eye with something."

"Same weapon," Wolf said. "Burning stick, hot end of a cigar. Doesn't matter. The man suffered. The work of a mindless animal."

Suddenly, Gabriel burst through the door with Cramer not far behind. "Father," the young man yelled, "I'm here."

Wolf stepped into the young man's path, trying to block his view. "Wait, Gabriel. No reason for you to see this."

Gabriel shouldered him aside, then froze when he saw Adam Laurent's prone form stretched out on the floor. "Oh, Father. Oh, my God. What did she do to you? No, no," he wailed. He knelt, sobbing, and placed trembling fingers on his father's forehead. "He was a good man. Gentle and kind. Just no match for Mother."

Wolf placed a hand on his shoulder. He never knew what to say when death visited. It seemed different folks needed to hear different words, so he said nothing and just let the young man sort out the reality of his loss. Finally, Gabriel rose to his feet. "Mother saw that he suffered before she killed him."

Wolf said, "You think she personally did this? Tortured him? Pulled the trigger?"

"All of it."

"We need to bury him, Gabe."

"When I was roaming the place yesterday afternoon, I came across a little family cemetery marked by a lone ponderosa on the hill north of the house. Half dozen graves—no more. It appears Angelina's parents and at least one brother are buried there. That's where he should be."

Mose said, "I can do some words, Gabe. I know my Bible."

Cramer said, "We've got some work to do. I'm going to give young Carl a shovel and let him help bury his friends and drag the bodies out of the house. I saw the Gomez brothers coming this way from down the valley. Gunfire probably caught their attention. They can help us. It will make them see how a wrong turn can end up. I don't think Carl will cause trouble, and I'm betting he's learned his lesson, Wolf, if you put him under my wing."

"I'll do just that. I can't haul him back to Santa Fe, and it doesn't appear he killed anybody. Try to make something of him. I would appreciate it, Woody, if you could find a place to bury those men some distance from the family plot." He turned back to Gabriel, who still stood above Adam's body, staring at a man whose voice he would never hear again. "Gabe, what about the cowhands that were killed when your mother brought her gang here?" Do you know where they're buried?"

"I never saw them. They killed most of them in the bunkhouse, and I wasn't there. They just disappeared. You can bet Beast and Hugo would have been too lazy to bury them."

"And the young woman—Consuelo I think was her name?"

Josh said, "Probably dumped them in a draw someplace. Might have pushed a few rocks over them. We can keep our eyes open, but they could be anyplace, and the buzzards and coyotes and other scavengers have probably done their work by now."

"You're probably right. We can make a search of the immediate vicinity later," Wolf said. "Let's get our work done. I'll want to see if I can pick up sign that tells me where they might be headed. We're not riding out today, but I'm going after them by sunrise tomorrow."

Chapter 31

JOSH RIVERS ACCOMPANIED Wolf as they rode into the foothills to pick up Lilith's trail. "Three riders," Wolf commented after his search about the soft ground of a watering hole.

"No surprise. Lilith, Raphael, and Jack."

"They're headed for high country. Going to avoid Santa Fe."

"Again, no surprise."

"We'll turn back for now. We need to get some things settled at the Bar P. I'll go after these people in the morning."

"You weren't planning to go alone?"

"That's how I had it worked out in my head."

"Well, revise your plans. I'm going with you."

"Jael wouldn't like it."

"And she wouldn't expect me to do anything else." He was confident when he said that. Their partnership went beyond a law firm and a marriage. They each accepted the other's independence. They might debate and express misgivings about the other's plans, but when one of them decided, the other backed the choice.

As they rode back down the trail, Wolf said, "You and Jael are a match, aren't you?"

"Yes, I guess you could say that. We never get tired of each other. I treasure every moment we're together. There's nobody I respect and admire more. I can't imagine anything that would separate us." He wished he could change his words when he remembered what Oliver was going through with Tabby.

"I thought it was like that with Tabby and me. I asked her to marry me before I left on my painting trip. Do you think that scared her off?"

"I suppose it could have triggered something. But she's a free spirit. Smart as a whip. Obviously, a gifted writer. I'm too conventional, I guess. I never could figure her out. But sometimes her emotional side overrides good sense."

"Would you wait for her if you were in my boots?"

"I'm her brother. I wouldn't give an opinion if I had one. I can tell you, though, that when I first met a Comanche woman who went by the name of She Who Speaks, the thought never crossed my mind we might end up married." He chuckled. "Doesn't mean I didn't want to bed that woman, though. But we had some hellish battles before we both gave in to the truth that we belonged together."

"Well, I got a few mountains to climb before I sort it all out, I guess."

After they stabled the horses, they strode to the house. "Smells better than when we were here this morning," Josh remarked as they approached the house. "I'm guessing fresh-baked bread."

When they entered, Josh saw that the others were already eating at the long table in the formal dining room off the kitchen. Mose stood at the woodstove in the kitchen and called, "Leftovers, gents. Roasted beef and beans. But I baked fresh bread and apple pies. Come in here and grab your plates and I'll dish up some grub."

They did not hesitate and soon sat down at the table with the others, including Cramer and his three hands, the thwarted outlaw eating with his eyes fixed on the table. Josh was pleasantly surprised to see that Gabriel was eating, but then it occurred to him the young man likely had not had a decent meal for hours given his imprisonment in the old cistern. Also, he had a hunch Gabriel had not been all that shocked to learn of Adam's death. He had likely calculated the odds given the effort to divert him from any contact.

Mose came in the room and sat down with his own plate. He looked at Wolf. "Where do we go from here, Marshal Wolf?"

"That's what we need to talk about. Woody, would you and your men consider staying on and running this ranch for Mrs. Laurent until legal things get sorted out? I'm guessing she's going to need a manager long-term. I'll put in a word for you, and I'll bet she will have a real opportunity for you here. All of you."

"I love this mountain country, and they ain't even touched the potential of this operation. Yeah, I would do that. I'd like for Mose to stay on, too. Supervise the cooking and the horses."

Wolf looked at Mose. "I'm thinking you and Woody have talked about this."

"Yep. I'm hoping the lady might let me build my own little cottage here and bring up a few of my own horses. Good stock that would help build the ranch. Gabriel's got to get word to his sister and stepmother. I thought we'd ride back to Santa Fe together, and I'd take that buckboard and a team and bring back supplies. Maybe hire another man and wagon if the boss-woman says okay.

We will have to take the wagon trail to Taos, so it will slow us up more than a mite. I might be able to leave the wagon in Taos if we can get supplies there, and then we'd ride on to Santa Fe horseback."

Josh said, "You wasted all that time worrying over this, Oliver. It sounds like a good plan to me."

"Not exactly how I had it figured, but, yes, I think this takes care of immediate concerns." He spoke to Mose. "Marshal Calder should be back in his office by now. Would you report what's happened? He has likely heard part of the story from Danna or Jael. Tell him that Josh and I are going after Lilith and the other two. See if he can send telegrams out to sheriffs or other lawmen in the territory to be on the lookout."

Gabriel said, "Oliver, it's not worth it. Let somebody else track them down. I want to see them brought to justice, but you need a posse. You don't know how dangerous they are. My mother and Jack are like a pair of water moccasins hanging in a swamp tree. You won't get a warning when they strike. Not like the rattlesnakes out here in the territory."

"I take them seriously. But it's my job. And if they get out of New Mexico, I think the law will play hell getting them back."

Josh thought Oliver Wolf had already done his job. He had removed the criminals from the Bar P. And there was nothing to be done for Adam Laurent. Oliver was only a temporary law officer. He was entitled to head back to Santa Fe and turn in his badge. But if persistence was virtue, Oliver Wolf was king of the virtuous. And Josh was committed to backing this good man.

Chapter 32

I T HAD BEEN a grueling four days. Tabitha knew Cal had travelled through the fires of hell, but it had not been an easy journey for her and North Star, as they stood watch and nursed her brother through sweats, chills, dry heaves, and hallucinations. Several times they had been forced to restrain Cal physically to prevent his lurching and screaming into the forest. But gradually he had calmed and stopped resisting water, and yesterday he had begun eating a bit. This morning he had been ravenous, devouring biscuits and venison strips and washing it down with several mugs of hot coffee. The old Cal was on his way back.

Cal was leading Smokey to the stream to drink when Tabitha eased in behind him. "Will you be up to travelling tomorrow?"

"I could have ridden today. I told you that."

"North Star said an extra day would be best."

"Is he boss man now?"

"Don't get testy. I don't know what I . . . we . . . would have done if he hadn't shown up. He has had experience with things like this."

"Like what?"

She couldn't think of a gentle way to put it, and she decided she was finished dancing around Cal's problem. "Like drying out drunks."

He stopped and turned toward her, his eyes sparking with anger. At least there was some life in those sky-blue eyes, something she hadn't seen for a spell. He opened his mouth to speak, but she cut him short. "There. I've said it. You're a drunk, Cal. But that doesn't have to be your future. Your choice. North Star says one drink and you are headed down the drunk road again. For some folks it can't be a matter of just cutting back or taking a drink now and again. They've got to quit the demon cold. North Star has seen this among his people, including his own father, and he believes you are one of those. Do it for those kids of yours. Maybe it could help with Erin. But most of all, do it for yourself."

Cal's fingers tightened on the gelding's reins and he chewed on his lower lip. Tabitha had expected an angry retort, but her brother was showing surprising restraint.

Finally, he spoke softly. "I need to finish watering the horses." He wheeled and picked up his pace as he led Smokey to the stream.

She returned to the camp, where she found North Star saddling his horse and loading his gear on his pack-horse. "Are you leaving?" she asked. "I thought you were riding with us to the Navajo homeland."

"I think it is time for me to disappear so you and your brother can make your peace. I will ride ahead and seek out a trail that will lead us through the mountains. I will be gone no more than three nights and will double back and tell you what I have found. If you ride west from here, you will find the Apache Trail. It goes all the way south to Albuquerque. There are good camping spots along that trail. It is well-travelled, meaning that trappers or traders might pass through every few weeks. Water and grass. You will know you have found it when you come to a trail wide enough that people can ride three or four abreast. The military opened it up when the Navajo made the Long Walk to the Bosque Redondo. The walk was far south of here, but the trail provided access to the north for cavalry chasing Apache or escaping Navajo."

"Your mother spoke of the Long Walk, and I have heard references to it. I wonder if there is a story there?"

"Many stories, I would guess. Perhaps our relatives will have some. It took place during and after the American Civil War. There should be survivors who carry the experiences in their hearts and heads. Anyway, if you will camp near the trail and wait, I will find you."

By the time Cal returned from caring for the horses, North Star had departed. Tabitha was scraping biscuit char from a Dutch oven when he walked over to her, knelt, and took the cast iron kettle from her hands. "I'll clean up, Little Sis. About time I got off my lazy ass. If we got some jerky and left-over biscuits to gnaw on to tide us over, I'll try to fix us a decent supper. I saw a can of apples with the supplies. Maybe I can make cobbler."

Tabitha gladly relinquished clean-up and cooking chores and stood up. "That sounds good, I could use some time to catch up on my notes."

"Where did your cousin go?"

She explained North Star's plan. "But I think his real purpose was to give us some private time."

"I was going to thank him and apologize. I owe him big."

"I think that would be nice."

"And I thank you, too, Tab, for seeing me through my bad behavior. I'm sorry for what I put you through these past days. I don't remember some of it, but what I do I ain't proud of. You won't regret it. This ain't going to be easy, but I decided to grow up. And when our little adventure's done, I am going to go back and do right by my kids, whatever happens between Erin and me."

Tabitha said nothing. She loved her brother and had done what she had to do. But Cal's remark about growing up had made her question her own behavior of late. She was beginning to feel a sense of shame and no small amount of regret about the way she had treated Oliver.

Chapter 33

DANNA AND JAEL sat in Danna's office discussing the Laurent case. They had learned of Adam Laurent's brutal end when Moses Monroe and Gabriel Laurent returned to Santa Fe the day before. Gabriel had broken the news to Margo and Angelina immediately after the men reported to the marshal's office.

"How are Angelina and Margo taking it?" Danna asked.

"I spent an hour with them last night, and we talked while Gabriel and Rylee prepared supper. Surprisingly, Margo was rather stoic about it all, although she was obviously distressed. One never knows how people will react to tragedy. And she may be stricken harder months from now. You and I can both relate to the tragic loss of parents. But I was so afraid when the Comanche took me and so focused on surviving, I didn't shed a tear over my loss until the reality that it was not just a nightmare struck several months later. Then I was inconsolable for a week."

"It took me a year. And, of course, the hurt and anger never go away, but I suspect Margo was somewhat prepared mentally for the outcome." Danna remembered vividly her obsession with escape when Comancheros raided the family farm and killed her parents and baby brother.

"Yes, that's likely. Angelina is taking it much harder, but she has the baby to distract her and feels that she still has a part of Adam with little Martina. It helps that Gabriel and Margo are so accepting of her. She is looking to Gabriel for a lot of guidance right now, and he does not seem the least intimidated by the decision-making. He is quite an impressive young man."

"Do you see him becoming a rancher?" Danna asked.

"I don't think so. Not hands on. Rylee says he is interested in the law, as a matter of fact."

"You don't think . . ?"

"It's a possibility. I think Rylee is blazing a trail for him. She can be devious. He seems very bright. I'm guessing that he might be ready to take the bar after a few years of reading the law during a clerkship."

"Let's think about it. Of course, we would have to consult with Josh."

Jael smiled, "I don't think that will be a problem. He won't even want to be bothered with it. I will feel much relieved when he and Oliver return, though. I wish he hadn't taken on that job."

"They can take care of themselves. I'm sure they will be back soon."

"Not soon enough to suit me."

"Rylee and Gabriel preparing supper together. Do I a smell romance cooking in the kitchen?"

"There is little doubt they are taken with each other. I just hope they don't rush things."

Danna laughed. "She's eighteen years old, Jael."

"I know. And I was a warrior's third wife by that time. But she has had so little experience with romance."

"And you had?"

"Okay. I was sold to Four Eagles for ten horses and sent to his tipi to share with two other wives who despised me. But I brought a hefty price."

Danna said, "Just teasing. Perhaps we should get on with discussion of our client's business."

"Agreed. So the titleholder of the Perez grant is deceased. Who inherits the land?"

"The good news is that Lilith LaCroix, or whatever her name is, is not a likely claimant. My investigating lawyer in New Orleans reports that there is not a marriage certificate for Adam and Lilith recorded there. That would not be conclusive, but the burden would be on her to come forth and offer evidence of a marriage. If she's charged with murder, she will be staying as far away from the courts as she can."

"Also," Jael said, "if she is captured and convicted of Adam's murder, she could not by law benefit from his estate. A not guilty verdict would open a possibility of a claim, but she would still need to prove a valid marriage."

"Angelina is certain Adam left a will in a metal box under the floorboards beneath their bed. Marshal Calder will accompany Gabriel and Moses Monroe back to the Bar P, and he will supervise a search for the will while he is investigating the scene. He hopes to meet up with Josh and Oliver there and take custody of some prisoners. Angelina is confident that the will gives the property to her outright, especially since it was hers to begin with. I think Adam honestly thought that he, as a man, and someone removed from the bloodline in the title chain would be better positioned to defend the grant. The opposite was true, of course."

"Men sometimes make foolish assumptions, and some women can be very naïve."

"Well," Danna said, "the Santa Fe League will be all over this during legal proceedings straightening out ownership issues. Somebody with the League's backing will take legal action challenging the grant."

"But why? What do they have to gain?"

"Thirty thousand acres that would revert to the territorial government for public or private sale to be purchased by selected members of the League for ten percent of market value."

"Can they be successful?"

Danna shrugged. "Sometimes I would just as soon draw straws as count on a court decision. But I think we've got a solid case. The Perez land came directly as a Spanish grant from the King of Spain, older than the Mexican grants that came later. Until deeded to Adam Laurent, the land was held continuously through generations of the original grantee's descendants. I am confident we can defend successfully, but litigation could take several years. I don't know if Angelina will be left with any cash as a result of Adam's death, but she may want to consider making a nominal cash offer early on. That might be enticing to a plaintiff faced with spending legal fees on a risky venture."

"Give in to extortion?"

"The word is 'settlement,' Jael. It eliminates risk of adverse outcome. Our client will save legal fees. And it makes problems go away. Allows people to go forth with their lives."

"I hope your settlements hold up better than Indian treaties."

"That's why you will handle all of our representation of the tribes. My settlement agreements prove to be less frustrating."

Chapter 34

LILITH, JACK AND Raphael had taken a deer trail leading deep into the mountains above the Bar P Ranch valley. Lilith worried that they might be followed, but there appeared to be only two riders approaching the ranch house when she decided they should hasten their departure. There had been something about the set of the men in their saddles and the caution with which they moved that told her the visitors were not making a social call. Thus, when Jack suggested they head for high ground, she readily agreed.

From their perch on a flat where the trail had widened before threading into the forest, they enjoyed a clear view of the ranch building site and the surrounding valley. She was confident no one had taken up their trail yesterday, but this morning, not more than an hour earlier, two riders, looking like crawling ants from this distance had emerged from the stable and headed in the direction of the path Lilith's party had taken. She had no doubt that these were the two strangers.

Jack stood beside her. "Our so-called gunfighters obviously didn't stop those men. I guess they bought us some time. But not enough. We don't know this country. Travel isn't the same here as in Louisiana. They'll catch up to us before we can get a straight shot at Texas."

"Just two of them. We're three. We've got them outnumbered. We can take them down."

Jack nodded at Raphael, who lay on a blanket in the shade. His cheeks and jaw were colored in hues of dark blue and purple and swollen to the size of a fat pumpkin. His twisted nose forced him to breathe through his mouth and reveal the missing and broken teeth that had once formed the smile that charmed Louisiana belles. Sometimes he spoke in barely understandable grunts, but his speech was improving. Regardless, Lilith was starting to find his presence annoying, more than once thinking she should have left him behind. He could barely stay in the saddle, and the forced rest stops were costing valuable time.

Lilith spoke in a soft voice. "We could leave Raphael. Those riders would not be trailing us if they were not lawmen. Otherwise, why bother? They would be stuck with him. They would have to take him in or bring him along. Either way, he slows them down."

Jack stared at her in disbelief. "You are serious, aren't you?"

"Well, it is something to consider."

"He is your son, for God's sake. We have never spoken of it, but we both know he is our son. We will not leave him behind. He might not hang. I don't think they can prove he killed anybody, but you don't know. But at the least he goes to prison. How do you think he would fare there? He does not stay behind. Get that insane idea out of your head."

Lilith was stunned. Jack was becoming increasingly rebellious lately. He had never spoken to her so forcefully, and she did not know what to make of it. "It was just a thought."

"Well, get rid of it. Here is what is going to happen. We have a good lead right now. They won't catch up with us in a full day's riding, but they will be gaining. We'll stay together for now, but by day's end, I'm going to find a spot where I can set up and wait. I want those lawmen on the downhill side of me, and I want some cover. There's no shortage of such places up here. I will wait and ambush them when they show up, hopefully kill them both—but certainly keep them pinned down to buy you and Raphael time. I will track you and catch up later."

"But I don't even know where I am at now. All I can see are deer paths to no place I want to go and trees and mountains."

"When I find the place, I will know, And I will send you off in the right direction. But your destination is Albuquerque. There you will find people who for a price will get you and Raphael home. By that time, he should be some help to you. You are resourceful. Once you get there, you will find those people, and they will not be able to resist your money or your wile. Before we even arrived at the Bar P, I talked with Hugo about a back door out, and he told me about the Apache Trail that cuts north and south through the mountains and then down to the foothills and into the desert-lands. It's wide enough for a wagon, and you can't miss it, if you just keep angling southwest from here."

She could not believe what she was feeling just now. She had long ago convinced herself she needed no man and that males were just tools for getting what she wanted. But the thought of separating from Jack out in the middle of this savage, unforgiving land terrified her, a feeling that had rarely visited during her lifetime. "I don't like it."

"I don't care if you like it. This fiasco was your idea. I warned you to let everything be. For once, you will do what I say."

She pondered killing the arrogant bastard, but she knew they could not escape the law without him. She would tolerate whatever necessary to get back home and the haven and counsel offered by Mambo Lucia.

They mounted their horses and followed the trail into the trees with Jack leading. The forest provided shade from the sun's sizzling rays, and they rode on a plateau-like surface all morning. They made good time, and the level ride was a welcome break from the steep, narrow trail they had negotiated a day earlier. They stopped when the sun told them it was a bit after high noon and ate the remains of the roast beef and bread.

Silence had prevailed most of the morning, Lilith pouting over Jack's assertion of authority and instructing Raphael to rein his horse in behind the lead rider's so distance would render it easier to ignore Jack, who finally broke the uncomfortable quiet. "Up ahead we climb again. No steep drop-offs or bottomless canyons. This path seems to wind between bluffs and cliffs and rock formations. The trail has been broken by something other than deer and other wild animals. Horses have travelled here for many years, I would guess, probably Indians before the mountain men came. It leads to someplace, and it's a good bet it will take you to the Apache Trail, hopefully in a few days."

Lilith snapped, "You're still hellbent on staying behind then?"

"They've got to be gaining on us, Lilith. I want to face them on my terms, and I think we are approaching a lot of good uphill ambushing positions."

"Why can't we all stay?"

"One can hide out better than three. We run a greater risk they'll spot us and be warned if we're all trying to conceal ourselves. And this way, if things go bad, I will have purchased you and Raphael more time, and I know I won't do worse than even the odds some. I intend to score two kills and catch up with you on the Apache Trail."

Jack made sense. But she hated this idea. Since they hit their teen years, they had never been apart for more than a day or two so far as she could recall. She felt her mere presence would protect him. They had always protected each other.

They mounted their horses, and this time she slipped in front of Raphael, who appeared a bit more alert since gingerly eating his simple lunch. She did not speak, but she felt a need to be near Jack for as long as time allowed.

The trail climbed gradually for several miles before the rocky grade became more challenging. "This is it,"

Jack said pointing to a cluster of boulders that formed a natural parapet not more than ten feet below what appeared to be the trail's crest.

He dismounted and led his horse up the path, stopping intermittently to sight the back trail below. Lilith led her white stallion behind him. When they reached the top, Lilith was pleased to see that the trail tapered more gradually on the downside and appeared to continue into the lower mountainsides. The sooner she escaped the high country, the better, as far as she was concerned, and she hoped to never see another mountain in her lifetime. "It is a choice spot," she admitted. "You can see them coming from half a mile away, and you've got the high ground. It might work."

Jack grinned. "You doubted me? Miss Lilith, I have no interest in suicide. I'm looking to live a good long time yet. I've got plans."

"Plans? What kind of plans?" His teasing side always eased her mind. It also made her want him. If Raphael were not standing ten feet away . . .

Jack took her hand and they led their horses away from Raphael, who did not even appear to notice. When they paused, he moved close to her so their faces were no more than a foot apart. He spoke softly and slowly, exaggerating his Louisiana drawl. "There's a lady I know, just recently widowed, and I was thinking I might ask her to marry me as soon as we get back to Louisiana."

Lilith was momentarily taken aback. "I didn't know you had someone. Who?"

Jack moved his head nearer and continued smiling.

"You mean us? Is this a proposal?"

"If you want it to be. We've been more than married all these years. Why not?"

She thought a moment and then shared her thought out loud. "Why not? Yes, I will marry you, Jacques Moreau. I would say it's about time."

He took her in his free arm and pulled her to him, so tight that she could feel his readiness, and it ignited her own desire. His lips devoured hers, and for a moment all thoughts were erased from her mind except her desperate hunger for this man.

Jack released her and stepped back, leaving her frustrated and half-angry.

"I love you, Lilith. I want you to know that. And don't you say anything. I know that you want me and that you will marry me. That's enough. Now, you and our son must go. I will catch up with you after I've done my work here."

Chapter 35

WOLF AND JOSH reined in their mounts and dismounted when the trail turned into the forest. They were travelling light with meager rations, having decided a packhorse would slow their pursuit. Josh retrieved the crusty bread and beef jerky, now two days scrunched in his saddle bags and split the noon allocation with Wolf. He calculated that Mose had packaged rations that would last two more days, so if they tracked Lilith and her companions much further, the return journey would be on empty stomachs.

"Looks like our friends stopped here, too," Wolf remarked. "Shod hoofprints scattered about. Somebody stretched out on the grass. Probably Raphael, if he was in as bad shape as Mose said."

"Do you think we're gaining ground?"

Wolf knelt and traced his fingertips over the edges of some of the track, performing some magic that Josh could not comprehend. But he knew the former Army scout was reading something in the reddish-brown dust.

"We're no more than a half day back," Wolf said. "If they don't pick up their pace, we'll catch up to them before nightfall. They have likely seen us from the high ground, so we should not assume we are going to surprise anybody. Question is whether they try to outrun us or make a stand someplace. We need to be pondering that. We'll see how things look mid-afternoon."

Their quarries were certainly making no effort to cover their trail, not that it would have done any good with Wolf on their tail, Josh thought. As they followed the path that snaked through the trees, he could see the broken branches and hoof prints in the soft earth without dismounting. He supposed, though, that given their unfamiliarity with the mountain range and the lay of the land, Lilith dared not try to slip off an established trail. He wondered if she had a destination in mind.

As if hearing Josh's silent question, Wolf slowed and spoke to him. "They're headed for the Apache Trail. They must have heard of it somehow. Most of the trails over this way intersect eventually with Apache. I connected with it once west of Santa Fe. It leads into Albuquerque.

Almost a full-fledged road by the time it gets that far south."

"I've heard of it. Dad and Nate used to use the trail to go to Albuquerque to buy breeding bulls from somebody down that way. Too rugged in the mountains to come back that route. They always returned by way of Santa Fe and took the trail north from there."

"If they make it to Apache, they'll be tough to catch, but we should find them before that."

Soon they emerged from the woods and the trail started a steep climb again. Wolf signaled another stop. "That's a single-file path in front of us, and those rocks along the edges furnish perfect cover for somebody setting up an ambush. We're going to be like rabbits going through a burrow with a hunter waiting at the exit. I don't like this. They've got the high ground and a perfect trap. They might not be waiting for us up ahead, but they would be fools if they didn't take advantage of the opportunity and I don't take this Lilith or Jack to be fools . . . either of them."

"Can we go off the trail and work our way above somehow and see if somebody is waiting up ahead?"

Wolf dismounted, "Let's take a look."

Josh joined him, and they walked along the edge of the incline that rose above the trail, seeking out a break in the rock that might lead to a lesser-used trail. "Too steep," Josh said, "but it appears to level off into a path of some kind about a hundred feet up. We can't get there with the horses, though . . . goats maybe."

"Can you get up there afoot?"

"I don't see why not. Loose rock and shale might make footing tricky, but worst that happens is that I slide back down. It's not that steep. I'm not going to drop off into a thousand-foot chasm if I slip. What are you thinking?"

"Well, I thought I would stay on this trail with Owl and lead your buckskin behind me. We can't move at more than a walk anyhow. If you take that Henry and stay above us and keep up, maybe you can spot anybody waiting. I'll try to keep an eye up your way, but my sight will be blocked some by the rocks and cliff walls. Wave if you see somebody ahead. If your view is cut off from me, fire a warning shot and find cover. We might catch them in their own trap. When this chute fans out, you can come on down and claim your horse again, and we'll continue the chase. If sundown comes first, I'll find a spot on the trail, and we'll make dry camp there till first light."

"You're the marshal, but I'm concerned you are setting yourself up as a nice target for somebody."

"You got a better idea?"

"Smart thing would be for us to turn around and head back to the ranch and then Santa Fe, but since neither of us is inclined to do that, I'd better take to the slope."

"When you make that rim, wave if you think you've got enough pathway to keep your footing on. If you do, I'll move on up the trail."

Josh nodded, removed his rifle from the saddle holster and started up the slope. As he had anticipated, the loose rock and shale made treacherous footing. The incline would have been barely challenging if not for that. He figured out quickly that a straight-up climb was a futile quest, but by angling his course and probing his feet for solid footing, he could inch his way up at what seemed to him to be a snail-like pace. In fact, he reached the lip of the upper trail in no more than fifteen minutes. He pulled himself up on the pathway and immediately noted it was wider than he had expected, ranging from as much as seven or eight feet in width to as little as three feet where the ledge had washed or caved away. It appeared to be a frequently used deer or mountain goat trail, although to Josh it seemed a trail to nowhere. He supposed eventually it dovetailed with another that led to water or grazing.

Josh waved at Wolf, signaling he expected to be able to negotiate the trail. The mountainside here continued to slope upward for some distance until reaching a rock wall that would have been impossible to scale. He would not need to worry about more climbing unless his path faded and died someplace ahead. Then his journey would more likely be down, not up.

Josh checked his lever-action Henry and chambered a cartridge. He remembered that Civil War vets used to talk about how the Henry, which held sixteen rounds in the magazine, could be loaded on Sunday and shoot for a week. If he required sixteen rounds today, they were going to be in serious trouble. At first, he walked slowly along the upper trail, trying to keep an eye on Wolf and procure a sense of his footing. The path was not as stable as he had anticipated, and he realized quickly he had not embarked on a carefree stroll. What worried him most, however, was that his view of the rider and horses was frequently obstructed by rock formations and craggy cliff walls. He worried that any ambushers might be hidden behind the blind spots and that he might fail to catch sight of a shooter soon enough to head off an attack.

Josh figured he had walked nearly three miles when he caught sight of the summit less than a half-mile distant. His own path started to angle sharply downslope, and he suspected it would dovetail eventually with the main trail. Since they were approaching the highest point on Wolf's trail, it appeared the concerns about an ambush had been unfounded.

No sooner had that thought passed through his mind than he caught sight of a flash of light from a cluster of rocks just below the trail's crest—like sunlight reflecting off metal. His eyes sought out Wolf on the trail below, but once again his view was blocked by a rock outcropping. He brought up his rifle to fire a warning shot into the air just as another rifle cracked and lead bored into his thigh and brought him down. The Henry beat him to the ground and started to slide off the trail and down the slope an instant before he grabbed it. He heard the exchange of gunfire from below and lay flat on his belly while he pondered his situation.

His thigh throbbed and hurt, but the pain was not unbearable. Not yet, anyway. He ran the fingers of his left hand down to his thigh and felt the blood soaking his britches. When he brought the hand back, he saw that it was painted crimson. He would be in no position soon to help anybody if he could not stem the blood flow. He pushed himself up and worked his body into a sitting position with both legs hanging over the trail's edge. He could only hope that the shooter was too occupied with Wolf to finish off his wounded prey. Perhaps he thought he had scored a kill and was now distracted.

He dug his penknife from his trouser pocket, opened the blade and began cutting one of the sleeves off his cotton shirt. He removed the tattered sleeve and tied it snugly about his upper thigh, where the wound was located. Satisfied that the blood flow was significantly eased if not stopped, he turned his attention back to the gunfire. As near as he could tell, the gunfight was at something of a standoff. The shooter had Wolf pinned down, but the rifle's crack when Josh was hit had likely warned Wolf to take cover and disclosed the attacker's position.

Josh stretched out on the path now and studied the scene below. He still could not see Wolf, and the gunfire had become sporadic. He could see the rock cluster where the shooter was hidden, and he was certain there was only a single rifle firing. His guess was that Lilith had moved on with her son, and her right-hand man—or whatever this Jack was to her—had stayed behind to kill pursuers or buy time.

Josh calculated that the spot where the ambusher was hidden was well within his rifle's range. But a man couldn't hit what he could not see. His position overlooked the gunman's nest, and Josh weighed the risk of standing up to get a view of the man and possibly a bead on him. It would force him to expose himself as a target again, but his wound left him in no position to participate in an all-night siege, during which Jack Moreau would likely slip away and set up again somewhere along the trail.

He lifted himself to his feet, his left leg trembling and resisting his weight. He had guessed correctly. He could see Moreau crouched behind some rocks. He raised the Henry and sighted the rifle. Moreau looked up and saw him and swung around with his own rifle ready to fire. Josh squeezed the trigger, and the Henry cracked. Moreau stumbled backward. Before he hit the ground, Josh's second bullet struck his target in the chest.

Josh's arms suddenly felt weak, and he dropped his rifle over the trail's edge, and it slid down the shale-slick slope. His head spun for only seconds before a shroud of blackness dropped over him, and he collapsed, tumbling off the trail and chasing his gun down the mountainside.

When his eyes opened, he saw Oliver Wolf kneeling beside him, his face grim with concern. Wolf pressed an open canteen to Josh's lips. "Drink, if you can. You need to drink and keep drinking what you can hold. You've lost a fair amount of blood. Then we've got to head back down this trail. It will be dark in an hour. I would like to get back through the woods to that wide flat where we stopped earlier. Build a fire, rest some and look at that wound before we decide what to do."

"Moreau?"

"Dead. Two kill shots, six inches apart. Luck doesn't do that. You weren't telling me the truth about your shooting abilities."

Josh gave a sheepish grin. "I guess I've been practicing more than I said. Getting ready to challenge Tabby and Jael to a match." Then he winced when he moved his leg, and a bolt of pain shot through it.

"I looked at the wound," Wolf said. "Bullet seems to be lodged deep down. I can't dig it out. Not here, anyway. We need to get you back to the Bar P. Woody was handy with battlefield wounds. Maybe between the two of us, we can do some good."

"The longer it's in there, the greater the chances of putrefying. But what about that crazy woman and her son?"

"To hell with them. Let the real law track them down. I was a fool to take off after them and drag you with me. You did save my life, though, you know. If Moreau hadn't shot at you and warned me, I would have come around that turn in the trail right into his gun. And he had me pinned down. If you hadn't taken him out, he'd have got away even if he didn't kill us first."

Chapter 36

WOLF REINED IN at the clearing and dismounted. There was no way Josh could dismount by himself. He was leaning forward in the saddle and grasping the saddle horn for balance, obviously in great pain and struggling to remain conscious. Josh had not uttered a single complaint beyond a grunt or a groan when they hit rough terrain and jarred his wounded leg, but Wolf could see his friend's condition was worsening. The bullet needed to be removed, but he had nothing but a skinning knife with which to probe and not even a flask of whiskey for anesthesia or cleansing the wound. Yet, time was critical. They dared not delay by spending the night here.

He untied Josh's bedroll from behind the buckskin's saddle and spread it on the ground. Then he helped Josh dismount and half-carried him to the blankets, where he eased him down. "We can't spend the night here," Wolf said. "We'll rest no more than two hours. You try to sleep. I'll stake the horses close enough to the stream that they can drink and graze. They haven't been pressed that hard today, and it's downhill all the way and we will be moving slower than I'd like anyway. It's turning to the chilly side already so the heat won't wear them down. I think they'll be fine. I'd like to make the ranch house by noon tomorrow."

"I understand. I'll try to do my part."

"I would like to hitch you to your horse and lead him behind me. That way you can doze if you feel like it and won't tumble off." Wolf did not add that he did not expect Josh to be conscious by the time they reached their destination.

Two hours later, horses and riders moved out of the clearing and took to the trail. They stopped briefly every few hours when they came to water. At each stop, though, Wolf found it increasingly difficult to force Josh to drink, and, by the time the descent was half completed, the lawyer-deputy was hovering on the brink of delirium.

At least the wound was not bleeding seriously. Wolf had found a clean shirt among his own personal items, shredding it for bandages and changing the dressings at every halt. Each time, the old dressings had been bloody from seepage, but there had been no indication that bleeding was profuse.

By midmorning Wolf could make out the hazy outline of the Perez hacienda on the horizon. Josh was unconscious now, and Wolf was constantly rearranging the rope bonds to keep him in the saddle. He unholstered his Peacemaker and pointed the gun skyward and fired three quick shots. He hoped that might catch the attention of someone at the ranch. He nudged Owl ahead and was relieved when he saw two riders moving his way from the ranch home site.

He was more relieved when he saw that the riders were Woody Cramer and Marshal Chance Calder. Neither man sat tall in the saddle, but he could not think of two he would rather encounter at the end of their trek down the trail.

Both men had their eyes fastened on Josh when they met on the wagon trail leading to the building site. Cramer nodded at Josh, who was slumped in the saddle with his head drooping against his chest. "It looks like you found them."

"We did. But I'm wishing we hadn't. Josh got the best of Jack Moreau but took a bullet in the thigh. Deep. I knew you were handy with bullets and arrows, and I had nothing to work with. I thought I'd best get him back here. Chance gives me a second old Army sergeant, so maybe between you, this fix can be turned around."

Calder said, "What became of the woman and her son?"

"Gone. Frankly, when Josh got hit, she moved way down my list of priorities. I decided I would turn this over to the real law." Wolf unpinned the marshal's badge on his shirt and tossed it to Calder.

Calder said, "Are you quitting on me?"

"Damn right. Take me off your deputy list for at least the next twenty years."

"I see you ain't in a talking mood. Let's see to your friend, and we'll talk later."

Chapter 37

"I DON'T LIKE this a bit," a grim-faced Woody Cramer said after removing the bindings and shearing off Josh's pantleg. "I was hoping I might just have you load him in a buckboard and head for Santa Fe. I'm afraid you would be hauling a corpse into town by the time you got there. Wound's already starting to fester some. That bullet has got to come out."

Josh was stretched out on the bed in the same room where the late Adam Laurent had been incarcerated and killed. Assembled in the room were Wolf, Marshal Calder, Cramer and Moses Monroe. Cramer had called Mose in because they were quickly learning that Mose was a virtual fountain of knowledge on a wide range of subjects. Cramer stepped back from the bedside and looked down at Josh, who was slumbering or unconscious. Wolf did not know which. He stood next to Calder, and Wolf noted that the two men were amazingly similar in stature, neither more than five and one-half feet tall, both probably mid-forties but trim and fit. Cramer was thicker through the chest.

Marshal Calder, who with his trimmed, salt and pepper moustache always looked like he had just stepped from the barber shop, asked, "What do you need to get started, Woody?" Calder had a Georgia accent and had served in the Confederate Army before switching to blue after the war and riding with Mackenzie in pursuit of the Comanche. Cramer had served with the Union, but the two former sergeants had become fast friends and established mutual friendships with Wolf during their joint service with Mackenzie.

"I don't like doing this. I've carved out my share of lead over the years, but ones buried this deep, I generally waited for the docs."

Wolf said, "But you say that's not an option."

"No, it ain't."

"I could do this, if you would like." It was Moses Monroe's mellifluous voice, calm and confident.

The others turned to the lanky black man. Wolf said, "You've removed bullets?"

"Mostly from Indians when I lived a dozen years with the Comanche. Sort of an unofficial medicine man. They thought I had special powers because of my black hide. Bullets don't care what color skin they go through or what color takes them out."

Cramer said, "Mose, you got yourself a job. Tell me what you need."

"I got whiskey in the kitchen and a nice collection of knives. Would be nice to find a few clean sheets, one to lay out the man's leg on and the other to tear up into bandages and such. And then someplace in this house has got to be a darning needle or two—would really like two. I would look in those rooms the ladies used to sleep in. I'll bet somebody's got a drawer full of sewing and mending stuff. I'll get some water boiling. Woody, I would be obliged if you would help out here. Oliver, maybe you and the marshal can take a stroll and talk law business."

Wolf smiled, relieved to turn the responsibility for Josh's care over to somebody else. "Mose, you will get no quarrel from me. And Chance and I do have things to talk about."

Wolf and the marshal strolled out onto the veranda and sat down on a bench. A cool breeze drifted across the porch, and the canopy shaded them from the sun's rays. It had been a spell since Wolf had enjoyed such comfort, as brief and illusory as it would no doubt be.

The marshal asked, "Are you going to tell me your story? I'm gone for less than a week and come back to find out you're off playing marshal, a bunch of folks have been killed, and a crazy woman seems to be at the root of it all."

"You talked to Angelina Laurent and Gabriel?"

"Yes. The woman is confused and beside herself. She had a baby girl, who is fatherless. Danna Sinclair sat in on our talk and filled in some of the blanks. It seems they are concerned about some men from the League trying to challenge the land grant, so the poor woman's got money and legal problems facing her. But this all caught her by surprise."

"But Gabriel should have given you some background on his mother."

"Yes, he was going to ride back with us, but his step-mother—if that's what she is—and sister need him in Santa Fe right now, and he seems to know nothing about the ranch operation. He doesn't appear to have any use for his mother. I guess you could say he hates her. Sad thing, ain't it? Hating the woman who gave birth to you."

"Yes, I guess it would be. Of course, it's understand-able since she murdered his father."

"Do you know what he said? This Lilith wants to turn into a wolf person. I ain't never heard of such a thing."

He chuckled. "Maybe that's why you didn't catch up to her. She turned into a wolf and ran off with a pack someplace."

"If you believe that, you ought to turn in your badge."

"So this man friend of hers that you killed. You just left him?"

"The buzzards or some other scavengers will get some nice meals out of him. I might have brought the body back if I had found his horse. I searched for the mount. It appears his horse broke loose when the shooting started. I would guess the animal will catch up to Lilith. Anyway, if he doesn't, he's free and has got a fair chance of making it to someplace that will take him in. Especially this time of year when the weather is decent. And for the record, I didn't kill Jack Moreau. Josh Rivers did it with two well-placed shots. Don't let his helpless law wrangler act fool you. He's a good man to have at your back."

"I always take somebody with the Rivers last name seriously, including that lady friend of yours."

Chance evidently had not picked up rumors yet of the state of Wolf's and Tabby's romance. "Yes, they don't come any better than the Rivers clan."

"Well, my problem is how we're going to catch the crazy bitch. Her son says she'll head back to New Orleans and that we'll play hell catching her and bringing her back for trial once she gets there. I've sent out telegrams to other marshals' and sheriffs' offices to be on the lookout. It's too late for me to head back up that trail you took and try to track her."

"Don't go after her with less than five men."

"Don't know where I'd go anyhow."

"She's likely going to hit the Apache Trail and may know something about it. But she would be too far ahead to either catch her or cut her off. I would have Albuquerque authorities keeping an eye out for a woman dressed in red. Of course, that won't do any good if she makes a change."

They were silent for a spell. Chance Calder was a good marshal, Wolf thought, and he had always respected the man as both soldier and lawman. Tough. Fair. Uncorruptible. Add realist to the list. He was needed in Santa Fe, and the man was not going to be riding off to chase Lilith La Croix unless he had at least a fifty-fifty chance of catching up to her. And the odds were not anywhere near that good.

Chapter 38

WOLF AND CHANCE Calder were both talked out and sitting silently on the bench when Woody Cramer opened the door and walked out onto the veranda. They both stood as if synchronized.

Cramer's smile gave Wolf's morale an instant boost. "Good news?" Wolf asked.

"Well, it's not bad anyhow. Josh ain't fit to jump in the saddle right now, but old Mose got the lead out. He told me to let you two know he's about finished. My God, the man could be a surgeon. Those old bony fingers moved like a concert violinist I saw back home once. Graceful, I guess is the word."

"Did he have trouble finding the bullet?" Wolf asked.

"Mose had to do more cutting than he wanted in order to widen the hole. That's when Josh woke up, and we had to get him liquored up some. Had to tie that wounded leg to the bed frame, and I had to hold the poor devil down. But did you ever see a Chinamen eat with chopsticks?"

"Yep," Chance said, "over at Chin's Chinese Eatery. A thing to behold. I stick with my spoon and fork."

"Well, that's what this was: a thing to behold. He took them damned darning needles and started dancing them around in that bloody hole he opened, and first thing I know he fishes out the bloody chunk of lead. It was buried deep, clear to the bone right at the front of the thigh. I don't think I could have got it without chopping his leg half off."

Wolf asked, "What's Mose doing now?"

"Well, he flushed out the wound with the last of the whiskey. And he packed it with a salve he brought back from town for horses' cuts. He took a few stitches but wants to keep it open some to drain and maybe pour some more whiskey in it if he can find another bottle and poke some more of his salve in the wound."

"Is Josh awake?" Wolf asked.

"Hell, no. He's dead drunk, and he's going to wake up with a head feeling big enough to eat hay with the horses. He won't even notice the leg."

"I can believe that. Josh is not a drinking man."

"I can't say the same, and I could use a snort myself right now."

Marshal Calder said, "Sorry, Woody. Sounds like any alcohol we can scare up is going for medicinal purposes."

Wolf said, "If you gentlemen will excuse me, I would like to go in and have a chat with Doc Monroe."

"Go right ahead," the marshal said, "and find out when we can haul Josh back to Santa Fe. I need to get back to town, but I'll hang on a day or two and ride with you if we can move him that soon."

Wolf went back in the house and found Mose sitting on a chair wrapping Josh's thigh with wide strips of a shredded sheet. Mose looked up when Wolf walked in and gave him a quick nod before continuing with his task.

"Is he going to be all right?" Wolf asked.

"Depends. I've done what I can for him. The rest is up to luck or the good Lord. Take your pick. Wound alone won't kill him. But there's always that devil putrefaction lurking out there. I guess the doctors are starting to call it 'infection' these days. Don't matter what you call it, that devil kills more folks than any bullets. Knew a man that died from a finger cut whilst whittling. I'd like to get him to a doctor in Santa Fe sooner than later."

"We can move him then?"

"Won't kill him. Might hurt him some, but we can cushion up his leg in the buckboard. I'd like to keep an eye on him for a spell, but I'd say you could head out with him come morning. I can't do more for him here, and a full-fledged sawbones might be able to work some other magic on him—depends on the Doc."

"I think he will want to see Micah Rand."

"Good choice. He took a turn as an Army surgeon. Patched a good number of bullet holes. They say he's a Quaker. Might be a God-fearing man. That won't hurt none."

Chapter 39

LILITH LA CROIX and her son, Raphael Laurent, sat by a small fire in a clearing a short distance from the Apache Trail. The sun had dropped behind the mountain tops an hour earlier, and Lilith savored the shroud of blackness that covered the forest, the calls and screeching of the night birds, and even the grunts and growls of the four-legged creatures that roamed in the surrounding forest. If she ever, with Mambo Lucia's guidance, transformed to wulver, she, too, would join these creatures in the darkness.

They would be forced to move south on the Apache Trail in the morning, probably depart before sunrise. Food supplies were running short and they needed to find a source for supplies or reach Albuquerque soon. She had no idea of the distance to be travelled, but the trapper they had encountered the previous night said it might take ten days or more. She hoped they might come upon a trading post or trapper's lodge where they might replenish their dwindling resources.

She noticed that Raphael had nodded off again. His continuing drowsiness was increasingly irritating to her, and while he seemed to be recovering physically from his brother's attack, his brain seemed addled. He had difficulty grasping her instructions, sometimes spoke with a stutter and struggled forming complete sentences. Hopefully this would pass with time. But if patience was a virtue, she freely admitted she lacked that virtue.

They had come upon the trapper at this campsite, which from the fire remnants and matted grass appeared to be many wanderers' favorite. The man had heard them coming and hidden in the trees at the clearing's fringe with rifle ready. But she had called out to him, announcing they came as friends, and upon hearing a woman's voice, the man had stepped out and waved them in. When she had dismounted, she noticed immediately that the trapper was about her height, six feet or a bit more. Perfect.

He was a rangy man, and the snug buckskins suggested his frame was sheathed with muscle. His face might have been a handsome one, but a scraggly, bushy, black beard covered any evidence of it. He had eyed her hungrily and moved uncomfortably nearer. She supposed a man out in these isolated parts without a woman got plenty randy, and she had no doubt what he wanted. She had considered the possibility of giving it to him but could not get past his rancid breath and body stench. Regardless, she had not discouraged him, and she and Raphael had shared a meal of tough venison that had a bitter taste suggesting it was on its way to decomposing. The burnt biscuits had been only slightly more edible.

Raphael had predictably dropped off to sleep after supper, and the trapper had offered to show her the trail and tell her about the water sources and camp spots along the way. She had walked with him to the Apache Trail which was less than a hundred yards from their campsite. As they returned, he had tentatively put his arm around her shoulders, and she had not protested. Neither did she when he touched her breast. They paused, and he pulled her to him. He pressed against her, and she could feel the man's tumescence trying to burst from his britches. The image his urgency created had triggered her own lust until the stink from his breath reached her nostrils again and reminded her of her mission. She had placed the teasing fingers of her left hand on his trouser front and, with her right, slipped her narrow-bladed knife from its sheath and drove it into his kidney. When he had

stepped back with horror-stricken eyes, she slipped behind him, pulled his head back and slid the razor-sharp
blade across the tender flesh of his throat.

Tonight, she still smelled the man, for she wore his
clothes. She had disrobed him and drug his naked body
into the woods. This morning she had washed his garments in the nearby stream, removing most of the blood
and much of the dirt and grime. She had hoped the sun's
rays might bake the buckskins to freshness. But the odor
lingered. She had tossed her own red-hued garments on
the fire, thinking that the law might be looking for a red-
clad woman. Dressed in her confiscated clothes and the
trapper's dirty, misshapen Plainsman hat, she hoped she
would be mistaken for a man at a distance.

The trapper—he had said his first name was Mac—
had left next to nothing to restore their food supply.
Lilith decided to keep the horse and mule. Possibly, she
could sell or trade the animals along the way. The trapper's mare was a yellowish-gray color with black mane
and tail and black stripe along the spine. The animal appeared sound, and her unusual coloring might interest
some prospective buyers. It appeared the mare was going to become a nuisance, because Lucifer kept trying
to mount it even though it was obvious from the mare's
resistance that the female was not in heat. She pitied her

white stallion, for she understood the frustration of unsatisfied lust. Perhaps she could sell or trade his services on occasion during their journey home. What horseman would not treasure a foal sired by the magnificent stallion?

Mac had also left her with a stack of bundled pelts. She had no idea what creatures had died for the harvesting of their furs, but she knew they represented value. She had funds to return to New Orleans, but she could not resist the prospect of a little profit on her journey. They would take the pelts and market them at first opportunity. With that thought Lilith snuggled into her bedroll, wishing Jack would show up soon. She would have welcomed him to her blankets tonight. A quick coupling would have been adequate. Nonetheless, she surrendered to deep sleep quickly.

Lilith woke up well before sunrise when she heard movement on the trail they had taken to the campsite. The rattling of shale and pebbles and the nickering of a horse. She crawled out of her blankets, shivering from the icy mountain breeze that nipped at her shoulders. She picked up her Winchester and stepped back into the shadows of the forest. She had thought about waking Raphael but decided he would be too noisy. Better to let him lie there where he could do no harm.

She waited, listening as the horse drew nearer. Perhaps it was Jack, but would he not have called out? Soon a horse's head peered into the clearing. Jack's sorrel gelding. For a moment, she was elated, but when the horse walked into the clearing and moved toward her, she saw that the horse's saddle was empty. Jack was dead.

Lilith felt as though a part of her had been amputated. She was swallowed by a vast emptiness. Tears would not come. She had not cried since the rape that she and Jack had avenged together all those years ago, and she would not surrender to tears now. She had never envisioned life without Jack, but she had her own destiny as a descendant of Adam's first wife, and she would go on, seeking to fulfill it until she drew her last breath. All she had left of Jack now was their pathetic child. Would he recover from his savage beating? Might he yet become a credit to the man who sired him and the mother who bore him? She must take him to Mambo Lucia when they returned to New Orleans.

Chapter 40

TABITHA WAS ENCOURAGED to see Cal hunkered down in front of the fire brewing coffee when she awakened. The aroma of cinnamon biscuits baking in the Dutch oven wafted her way, and she scrambled out of her bedroll and stuck her head out the front of her pup tent. She watched Cal lift the lid off the oven with a notched stick he had obviously sculpted for that purpose. The lid was covered with hot coals, and half as many lay under the oven. Management of the heat was the key to Dutch oven cooking. Put the oven on an open fire, and unhappy diners would be eating charred remains of the contents.

She knew Cal to be a fussy cook and an accomplished one when he chose to be. Lately he had not been choosing and had to be nagged out of his bedroll in the mornings. She would welcome his returning to morning camp chore duty. She crawled out of the little tent and got up and disappeared into the woods to pee. After washing up in the ice-cold stream, she joined her brother by the fire, finding its heat more than welcome. "This is a nice surprise," she remarked. "Biscuits smell scrumptious."

"I made plenty. We'll have extra to carry over for a few meals along the trail. I figure North Star will be back tonight, and we'll have another mouth to feed tomorrow. Do you want bacon?"

"No. Save it. Cinnamon biscuits and coffee are enough."

"Figured it was time for me to start earning my pay."

"Who said you were getting paid?"

"I'm not?"

"I am furnishing the supplies. All I promised was adventure."

"I'll keep my eyes open for business opportunities along the way. Maybe I can get into the whiskey business."

Tabitha gave him a cold glare. "That's not funny."

"You never did have a sense of humor, Little Sis. Too serious. Like our ma."

She did not argue the point. Aurelie Rivers, the mother who raised her, was like that—stern and taciturn. Pretty, but dour faced, although quite stunning on the rare occasions her happy face appeared. Aunt Dezba had told her that Summer, the mother who gave her life, was a constantly smiling, cheerful person, something of a jokester. Tabitha had to admit she might take life—and herself—too seriously sometimes. She did not laugh a lot. Jael could make her laugh, sometimes hysterically. And Oliver. She had not thought about it before, but he would tolerate a somber mood for only so long before he would tease her out of it. Now that she looked back, she laughed a lot when she was with Oliver.

They sat close to the smoking embers of the dying fire and finished their biscuits. She poured more coffee in her tin cup and offered to fill Cal's, but he waved it away and pressed a finger to his lips. "Hear that?" he asked in a soft voice.

She listened and whispered, "I don't hear anything."

"That's what I mean. The birds have gone quiet, and the squirrels and chipmunks ain't chattering. Somebody's coming down the trail—probably nobody bringing trouble, but it wouldn't hurt to have our guns close by. Why don't we just move back in the woods a ways until we see who's coming?"

Not more than ten minutes later, Tabitha heard the whinnying of horses and the pounding of plodding hooves approaching slowly from the north on the Apache Trail. Soon, a rider sitting-military erect in the saddle astride an impressive white stallion appeared. The rider's attire of ragged buckskins and a too-large hat supported by the wearer's ears somehow seemed incongruous to bearing and mount. He reined in the stallion and looked in their direction, obviously attracted by the smoke. Another rider joined him, followed by a string of several horses and a mule loaded with stacks of pelts that were on the verge of slipping off its back.

The white stallion's rider nudged his horse through the brush toward their campsite. "Hello, the camp," the rider called. At that instant, Tabitha realized that the long black hair tumbling from beneath the hat belonged to a woman.

Tabitha waited for Cal to take the lead, and, momentarily, he stepped into the clearing, his rifle pointed down in one hand and waving with the other. "Hitch your horses and come on in," Cal said. "Coffee's hot, and we got fresh cinnamon biscuits you're welcome to share."

The strangers tied their horses near the trail and came down the short path leading to the campsite. Tabitha stepped out to greet the visitors and noticed the woman took the lead when they approached the campfire. A young man with a face nearly covered with purple and yellowish bruises followed like a wary pup. He had a

Colt slung low on one hip. What a strange pair to be out in these mountains trapping for furs.

The woman's attire said she was a trapper. Her bearing and manner certainly contradicted any stereotype, and her companion did not look like one accustomed to the rugged life. Their dark skin suggested mixed racial heritage, but the tint was different than that of the many white and Indian or Mexican mixed-bloods of the southwestern United States. When the tall woman pushed her hat off her forehead, Tabitha confirmed that the visitor was stunningly beautiful.

"I am Elizabeth Carter," the woman said, moving to Cal and extending her hand and holding his grip much longer than Tabitha thought necessary while she made eye contact. "And this is my son, Richard."

Richard nodded but remained well behind his mother.

"I'm Cal Rivers. Pleased to make your acquaintance."

Tabitha might as well not have been there, she thought. Cal and this Elizabeth were each appraising the other in a way that could only lead to trouble. Since Cal was not going to introduce her, Tabitha said, "And I am Tabitha Rivers."

The woman turned her head to Tabitha but did not step away from Cal. Then she spoke to him. "A wife?"

Tabitha took it that a wife would be a mere inconvenience to what the woman had in mind. "I am his sister."

"That's nice," the stranger said, and, again, speaking to Cal, "the coffee and biscuits would be very welcome. We didn't eat this morning. I fear we are running short of food supplies."

"Set yourself down on those stumps next to the fire. I'll toss a few more logs on the coals and then fetch extra cups from my tent."

The visitors sat down, but Tabitha remained standing. Something was not right about this pair. "Where have you been trapping?" she asked.

"Oh, up in the mountains."

The vaguest possible response. She decided to address the young man, who had yet to speak his first word. "Do you like trapping, Richard?"

He looked uncertainly at his mother, who gave a slow nod. "Uh, yeah. I g-g-guess."

"What do you mostly trap?"

"Uh, uh, animals."

What in the hell else would he be trapping? "I mean what kind? Beaver? Otter?"

Elizabeth Carter intervened. "Please don't question my son. As you can see, he suffered a terrible fall several days ago and injured his head badly. He is not thinking clearly yet and does not handle questions well."

As a writer, Tabitha was conscious of people's speech patterns and grammar usage, and this woman obviously hailed from the deep South, was well educated and a person of monied background. She did not earn her living as a trapper.

Before she could probe further, Cal returned with the cups and began pouring coffee for the unexpected guests. Then he lifted the lid off the Dutch oven. "Biscuits are still warm. Help yourselves."

Elizabeth Carter plucked two from the oven and handed one to her son, who now had a biscuit in one hand and a coffee cup in the other. He devoured the biscuit in two bites and looked questioningly at his mother. Cal picked up on his silent inquiry and put the Dutch oven at the young man's feet. "Eat till you are filled up, Richard. Would you like another, Mrs. Carter?"

"Perhaps one would be nice . . . but, please, call me Elizabeth." Cal speared a biscuit with a fork and handed it to her just before her son started wolfing down the remaining biscuits. *So much for the surplus*, Tabitha thought.

Tabitha continued to stand, but Cal knelt on one knee across the fire from the raven-haired woman. She noticed Elizabeth Carter wore a holstered pistol on one hip and a sheath knife on the other. Tabitha sometimes wore her Smith & Wesson revolver when anticipating danger and almost always carried her knife when on the trail, but it made her wary of this woman and she was not about to put her Henry aside.

Cal said, "Elizabeth, those furs are about to slip off the mule. Before you move on, I can snug them up with diamond hitches so they don't drop off along the trail."

"That would be kind of you. I just don't know much about such things. I must confess that I am not really a trapper. These were my late husband's furs. Richard and I went out with him this trapping season—he had a cabin up in the mountains, where we stayed. But a few weeks back, he had a run-in with a bear and lost. He died a horrible death and now I am a confused widow. I never handled the business end of his trapping and don't know what to do with these damnable things. We just want to get to Albuquerque. If you are headed south, perhaps we could ride with you."

Tabitha observed that the widow seemed to be past her grieving, and the way she was working Cal with those dark eyes, it seemed she was ready for a new man to share her blankets. And, knowing her brother, he would probably be a willing partner. Tabitha was tired of this witch pretending Cal was the only Rivers in the camp. "We are not going south," Tabitha said tersely. "We are headed west, and our destination is the Navajo homeland. We will be passing through Apache tribal areas along the way. If you are seeking civilization, you will not find it where we're going. You're on the right trail to civilization . . . well, Albuquerque is half-civilized anyway."

The Carter woman did not even turn her head toward Tabitha and continued to ignore her presence. "Cal, I really do not want to take these furs all the way to Albuquerque."

"There will be trading posts once you get out of the mountains—five or six days, no more than a week."

"Would you consider buying the furs and the mule and the strange-colored horse? I'll sell at one-half market plus five days' food supplies for Richard and me."

"I wouldn't feel right taking advantage of you, but the furs and extra animals will slow us down, and I don't know where we'll be able to market anything. I'm sure I would have to take a heavy discount."

"And we can't spare five days' food supplies," Tabitha interjected.

Cal sighed and spoke to the visitors, "Let me confer with my sister about this." He got up and waved for Tabitha to follow him to the edge of the clearing where their tents were pitched. "Little Sis, I've got most all of my life's cash accumulation in gold double eagles in my saddlebags. This is a business opportunity. You ain't paying me for this trip. This is a chance for me to turn a profit, and you ain't got the right to stand in the way of it."

"Maybe you would just like to ride along to Albuquerque with the poor widow lady."

"I thought about it. She's a mighty handsome woman, and I don't think it's safe for her to be travelling all that way alone. Somebody's apt to take advantage of her. And I ain't talking about money. That young feller ain't right in the head, and he won't be any help if trouble comes her way. You don't need me all that much since North Star showed up."

"Cal, I appreciate your coming with me. I really do. And you will be needed in the days ahead. I want you to go with me, but you're a grown man and can do what you want. This woman will not be a path back to Erin and the kids, though. I'll bet on that. She's not from around here, and I don't see her staying anyplace close by. Her whole story stinks as far as I'm concerned. We can't spare five days' rations for two. I'll break out enough for two days and they'll have to stretch it."

"But there's plenty of game. We won't go hungry."

"She's armed to the teeth, if you haven't noticed. I've got a hunch she knows how to use that rifle she's got in her saddle scabbard."

"Are you okay if I make a deal for the furs and animals?"

"Go ahead. They won't slow us that much. Somewhere there is bound to be a trader who will take the furs off your hands. Send Richard over while you and the woman go look over the merchandise and do your dickering. He can help me sort out the food supplies and carry them to their horses. I want them out of here now."

"I just don't understand why you are so damned unfriendly and hostile about Elizabeth."

"You don't understand because she's got you under her spell."

Cal shook his head in disgust and walked away, stopping at his tent to pick up his saddlebags. Tabitha went to the tarp-covered stash of food supplies near her own tent. She started sorting out a few cans of beans and fruit and a small sack of flour for the Carters and put them in a large cowhide bag. She grudgingly surrendered token portions of ham and bacon but was more generous with the jerky with which they were oversupplied.

She started when Richard came up behind her and spoke, "M-M-Mother said I should help you."

Ron Schwab

Tabitha straightened and turned. "Richard. I didn't know you were there."

"Name's not R-R-Richard. My name is Raphael. Raphael Laurent. Mother f-f-forgot, I guess."

"Oh. And I forget your mother's name."

"Lilith. Her name is Lilith. We were playing a game, she said. Maybe I shouldn't have said anything."

"Well, why don't you take this bag over to your horses. I'll be right along."

Raphael slung the bag over his shoulder and walked away on unsteady feet headed for the horses. Tabitha retrieved her rifle from the pup tent, where she had put it down. She levered a cartridge into the chamber and crept through the forest until she came up behind Cal and Lilith. She listened to Cal talking to the woman. "This mare is called a bayo coyote here in the Southwest—a yellow dun with a black stripe along its spine. I would give you full price for her—one hundred dollars. I can't do more than twenty dollars for the mule. The furs might bring a thousand or somewhat more at a big trading house. I'll give you four hundred. That would be five hundred twenty dollars for the lot."

"Agreed."

Cal lifted his saddlebags off his shoulder, knelt on the ground and opened the flap and began to count out

{310}

twenty-six double eagles. Lilith's fingers inched toward her holstered pistol.

Tabitha hollered, "Your fingers touch that pistol, Lilith, and your son is an orphan."

Lilith turned, and her smoldering eyes met Tabitha's, which were sighted down the Henry's barrel. "What are you talking about? I wasn't doing anything."

Call stood up and looked at his sister with annoyance. "Little Sis, lower that rifle. Elizabeth and me are just doing a little business."

"Her name isn't Elizabeth. Finish your business. Then they've got five minutes to get the hell out of here. My rifle stays put till they're out of sight."

Lilith accepted the money and dropped it in a doeskin pouch. "It was a pleasure doing business with you Cal. I wish we could have become better acquainted, but your sister appears to be a possessive sort."

Cal helped saddle the horses and gave a friendly goodbye wave as Lilith and Raphael rode on down the trail. True to her word, Tabitha did not lower her rifle until the last puff of trail dust feathered away.

"Little Sis, I just can't see you treating our guests that way."

"She lied about their names. The son told me. And she was going to draw on you and blow out your brains and take your money. She figured I would be easy to deal with."

"Lots of reasons folks out this way don't use their real names. That don't mean anything. And you were mistaken. She wouldn't have drawn on me. I can't imagine that sweet lady hurting a soul."

Chapter 41

J OSH RIVERS LAY in one of the beds at the Rand Clinic while Dr. Micah Rand examined him. He had spent two nights in the clinic and was ready to vacate the premises. Rand had promised he would be released this morning if he found no sign of infection in the wound. The young physician had completed closing the wound the previous afternoon and was redressing it now.

"You are healing nicely," Rand said. "No sign of infection. Moses Monroe did a masterful job. I had no idea he was a skilled surgeon."

"There is probably something Mose can't do, but I haven't discovered it yet."

There were several soft knocks on the doorframe, and Jael stepped in. "What's the verdict, Micah? Can I haul him home?"

"Yes, and you can take him back to the office tomorrow."

"That would please Danna."

Rand smiled. "Yes. I have had to listen to her grumbling. That's why I wanted to make it clear. Now, I have patients waiting. I'll turn this one over to you, Jael."

"My pleasure."

After Doctor Rand left the room, Josh inched his wounded leg over the side of the bed and sat up. "I guess I'd better get into those clothes you dropped off yesterday."

"Yes. Then I'll take them off when we get home. This is Michael's last school day. I thought we could take advantage of his absence before I go back to the office."

"Are you serious?" He suddenly found himself hoping so. "We'll have to be careful."

"Oh, I'll think of something. You do realize, don't you, that if that bullet had hit six inches to the right, we wouldn't be talking about this?"

"I hadn't thought about it."

"Think about it and be grateful. I am," Jael said.

"You can be coarse sometimes, you know."

"And you love it."

He looked up at her, smiled and winked.

"Get dressed. I'll get your cane. I left it in the hallway."

"Cane?" He had pulled his shirt on by the time Jael popped back in the room.

"Hand carved from cherry wood. Very nice. Rylee picked it up from Spiegelberg's. She thought it was very elegant and that you would look distinguished using it. Perhaps you will want to continue wielding it for appearances after you don't need it anymore."

"Don't bet on it. How about helping me get my britches on?"

Jael helped slip the denim trousers over his feet and knees, but he had to stand to tug the fabric over his thighs. Josh had to rest his hands on her shoulders while she finished the job. "Hey, what are you doing?" he asked.

"Checking to see if it still works."

"It obviously does. What if somebody came in here?"

"I hadn't thought about that. If a woman saw what's down there, I would have to chase the women of Santa Fe off with a stick to keep them away from you."

He slipped into a pair of moccasins, and, with Jael's support, hobbled out to the carriage. He managed to climb in without undue difficulty, and Jael stepped up and took the horse's reins.

"Bring me up to date," Josh said as the buggy rolled out of town and pulled onto the trail that would take them the several miles to their house. "Any word on Lilith La Croix?"

"Nothing. Gabriel is betting she makes it back to New Orleans. If she does, it will be a challenge to arrest her and extradite her back to New Mexico Territory. Incidentally, subject to your approval, Danna wants to offer Gabriel a clerking position with the firm. He'll read the law while he works for us and eventually take the bar examination. Danna says he is very bright."

"I'm certain my approval is just a formality."

"Well, he has been working in the office several days now."

"We can see how it works out. It would be nice to have another male in the office. What about his sister and the new baby and stepmother . . . if that's what she is?"

"They and Gabriel are going to stay with Oliver for at least the next several months, maybe longer. Eventually, Angelina will move out to the ranch with the baby, and I suspect Margo will, too. But Woody Cramer and Moses Monroe will run the place till all the legalities are worked out and probably indefinitely."

"And tell me about the status of the legalities."

"We think as far as New Mexico Territory is concerned, we can establish Angelina and Adam were legally married. Danna plans to seek a declaratory judgment to that effect from the court. Since Lilith will be in no position to challenge, that should be routine. Next step will be to probate the will that the marshal recovered during his search of the house. That left the ranch to Angelina. While that is being completed, we will focus on heading off any attempts by the League to challenge the land grant."

"I hope we've got a paying client."

"Angelina is not land poor. She did have substantial cash in the bank that she wisely held onto when she deeded the land to her husband. The lawyers will get paid."

"Maybe she is smarter than I was giving her credit for."

"Angelina will be just fine. And she will not be deeding her land to any future husband."

"I hope Oliver can get some work done with all those folks staying in his house."

"I think the company may be good for him, and they won't cause extra work. They've already taken over the domestic chores. Gabriel is even looking after the horses . . . with Rylee's help, of course. Their story remains to be written."

"I'm more concerned about Oliver and Tabby. I guess she will be back sooner or later."

"Yes, she will return with more stories to write. And I am guessing she will have a new appreciation for the man she left behind."

"I hope so. But will he wait for her?"

Acknowledgments

A special thanks to Ray Sarlin, who provided Summer Webb's backstory.

Made in the USA
Monee, IL
28 August 2022